THE PEOPLE OF NANT Y GRO CHAPEL

BY
O. MADOC ROBERTS

Translated from the Welsh by
GLYN LASARUS JONES

First published by the author in 1914 as Pobol Capel Nant y Gro
This translation first published in 2017 by Alan Roberts, Bristol, UK
English translation copyright © Glyn Lasarus Jones 2017
The rights of Glyn Lasarus Jones to be identified as the trans-
lator of this work have been asserted in accordance with the
Copyright, Designs and Patents Act 1988.
A CIP catalogue record for this book is available from the Brit-
ish Library.
ISBN-13: 978-1546701408 (CreateSpace-Assigned)
ISBN-10: 1546701400
Cover photographs: the Wesleyan Sunday School, Carno (ca.
1885) and the Elders of the Calvinistic Methodist Chapel, Ne-
fyn (1896) are from the John Thomas Photographic Collec-
tion and are reproduced by permission of Llyfrgell Genedla-
ethol Cymru/The National Library of Wales; the Chapel in
Nefyn by Alan Roberts.

ORIGINAL PREFACE

Some of these chapters first appeared in one of the oldest monthly periodicals of Wales. At the request of many of that periodical's readers, they are published in this format, along with many additional chapters.

The book is a simple attempt to portray life in Nonconformist Wales during the last fifty years, as far as I was given the opportunity to see it and to hear about it.

O. Madoc Roberts   *Conwy, St David's Day, 1914*

PREFACE to TRANSLATION

I don't think any of O. Madoc Roberts (1867 -1948) grandchildren or descendants can read Welsh, so we have had his book translated. It is based firstly on his experiences growing up in the Wesleyan Methodist community of Porthmadog in North Wales where his father was a ship's captain and his grandfather a farmer nearby in Talsarnau. Later experience and stories came after he studied at Didsbury College, Manchester to become a Methodist Minister. As a preacher he served first in Abergele and then throughout North Wales. In 1917 he was made Book Steward of the Methodist Bookroom in Bangor where he lived and was elect-ed Lord Mayor in 1937. The book is about the lives of people associated with a fictional chapel in North Wales in the fifty years before 1914.

Many chapters of this book were first published in a Welsh periodical called Yr Eurgrawn. When this was first published in 1809 it was called "The Wesleyan Magazine" but this was later shortened to "The Magazine".

There are many people to thank for their contributions to this translation project. Special thanks go to our translator Glyn Lasarus Jones who has brought the book to life in English. At an early stage Amy Sullivan, Chris Ousey and Meg Bailey advised and encouraged. Leonie Jones provided important inspiration through her documentation of Roberts family history. Richard Wright has edited nearly the whole book. My wife Joanna has supported the whole project, advised on the cover design, and given editorial advice on some chapters.

I have enjoyed being transported to another age and set of beliefs and hope that others will also enjoy getting to know the People of Nant y Gro Chapel.

Alan Madoc Roberts   *Bristol, 2017*

TRANSLATOR'S NOTE

It was a great honour to be commissioned by the family of the late Rev. O. Madoc Roberts to translate *Pobol Capel Nant y Gro* into English.

It was an especially challenging commission, particularly as *Pobol Capel Nant y Gro* is so very Welsh. Not only is the book Welsh in its idioms and expressionisms, it is also Welsh in its ethos, its characters and the life it portrays. Furthermore, it offers a glimpse into a

Wales that has long disappeared – a monolingual Welsh speaking Wales where the chapels held sway, and where ordinary people discussed literature, politics, theology and matters of the soul as a normal part of everyday life. Trying to render this authentically into English has been extremely difficult.

Pobol Capel Nant y Gro was exceptionally popular when it was first published, as reviews in the Welsh language newspapers of the time testify. It was also of course a means for the Rev. O. Madoc Roberts to convey his social teachings and his profound and beautiful theology.

Perhaps one of the most confusing issues for non-Welsh speaking readers will be the frequent use of Welsh house names. It was the custom in Wales, to refer to someone by the name of their house, often even without a first name, so "George Huws the *Pandy*," "the son of the Llwydiarth," or "the lady of Ty Newydd" are common in the book. Translating such names would have been impossible so I have simply left them as they are.

I would like to thank. Alan Roberts and Richard Wright for proofreading the translation. Their comments have been invaluable and the resulting dialogue has greatly improved the work.

I hope that reading this book will be as fascinating as translating it was. I can only hope that I have done justice with this most remarkable work of fiction.

Glyn Lasarus Jones   *Blaenau Ffestiniog, 2017*

CONTENTS

CHAPTER I

THE PEOPLE AND THE BARON

"Do you know what," said Captain Wiliams, captain of the "Angharad" to Sam Puw and Shon Gruffydd as they made their way unhurriedly but in good time to the seiat [1] at Nant y Gro Chapel one summer's evening, "I think it was a terrible mistake building this old chapel in such an inconvenient place. Why on an earth did the old fathers build it in such a remote location, was it a lack of sense or a lack of money?"

"Do you know, I've been thinking the same thing exactly, Captain", said Shon Gruffydd "I've heard that people used to refer to the old chapel as 'the old barn'. And I'll say this, it's much more convenient for the surrounding cows and sheep than it is for the villagers."

"Yes, yes, it's easy to find fault with the old fathers," said Sam Puw with his usual tact, "but I can assure you the location wasn't down to a lack of sense, nor the structure down to a lack of taste."

"Well what was the reason then, Sam Puw?" they both asked.

"We must remember to start with," said Sam Puw "that it was impossible to get land on which to build a chapel as the gentry had great opposition to the chap-

---

1   Seiat - an important fellowship meeting held in Welsh Nonconformist Chapels where members would pray, discuss matters of the soul and bear witness to God's work in their lives.

els, and because most of the Nonconformists in those days were ordinary people, and many of them had little means. Establishing the cause would read like a romance if someone familiar with its history were to write it. Just look at the advantageous location given to the State Church in every village, they usually stand in the centre of the village whilst the chapels even in the towns are excluded from the high street, and in the townships are banished to some remote corner out of everyone's reach. I often heard my father mentioning the trouble they had building the old chapel. He, along with some others, had the privilege of carrying stones to the site, and the only reward he received for his labour was a summons to leave the farm were his family had lived for at least two generations. Many received similar treatment, beside him."

"Who owned the land, Sam Puw?"

"Oh! Baron Owain, a kind enough old gentleman if he had his own way. The old Baron's main flaw was his zeal for the Church and his hatred of the chapel. His zeal and hatred stemmed from the same feeling – they were one and the same and each as blind as the other. He was asked more than once for convenient land on which to build a chapel, but he adamantly refused, saying there was enough room for everyone in the church, and that's where everyone should go. Owain Wiliams, *Cae Glas*, daringly suggested 'that there's enough room in hell too, but they didn't want to go there,' and the old brother suffered greatly for speaking so plain."

"How did they succeed in the end, Sam Puw?"

"Well, you see, as it happened, Lloyd, master of the *Henblas*, a zealous old Nonconformist, owned a plot of land outside the village, and through the influence of the minister of Shiloh, Caerefron, the land on which the current chapel stands was secured. So it was necessary to build the chapel where it is, or do without. But remember, many of the old Nonconformist fathers had been worshiping from house to house before the chapel was built. I often heard my father saying how the old minister of Shiloh faced many a terrifying skirmish trying to establish a cause here. Paul mentions somewhere that the marks of the Lord Jesus were even on his own body. The old minister of Shiloh could say that similar scars where on his body too, because he was set upon more than once when visiting this village. My father and some others had to escort him home many a night because some of the old enemies of Nonconformity were threatening to molest him. Yes, the old people suffered tremendously whilst establishing the cause, but the old barn, as the old chapel was derisively referred to, proved to be God's sanctuary to the godly old saints. They preferred climbing the hill to the small chapel, and paying for the Gospel from their frugal means, rather than benefit from Mr Vaughan the Parson's free ministry. Remember, this wasn't down to any bad feeling towards the Vicar or the Church, but a genuine thirst for the Gospel. The Vicar, from what I heard, was a gracious enough man, but was more interested in his gun and fishing rod than in his parishioners; his wife and the Baron's daughter were the small chapel's arch enemies."

"It's a great pity that someone wouldn't write the history of how the cause was established," said Shon Gruffydd. "I'm sure you could write chapters as interesting as those in the Book of Acts. I remember this minute how my mother would tell the story of old Shon and Mari Llwyd, how they toiled up the hill towards the small chapel. As they advanced in age the hill became a greater burden, and the breath of the old sister became shorter. This is how they talked on the village hill":

"Isn't it terrible, Shonyn, how people couldn't have a plot of land nearer the village on which to build a chapel to the Owner of all things. You can get land anywhere to build a tavern, but when land is needed for a chapel".

"Before she finished her sentence, (and it took some time I would have thought for the old woman to complete her sentences when climbing the hill), Shon Llwyd said: 'Don't you worry, Mari, God will raise up lads in Wales soon enough you'll see, who will go to that Parliament and set those bigwigs straight.' 'Amen' said the old lady, planting her stick in the ground to help her recommence her steps. It's no wonder that the old brother, after arriving at the chapel, referred to the Baron in his prayer. 'Great Lord', said the old brother, 'you are great, you are greater than Baron Owain, and thank goodness for that! You don't need help from anybody. And if you did, you wouldn't get any from Baron Owain, that's for sure. It's good for him that you are God and not I."

"What surprises me", said Sam Puw, "when you consider how much persecution the chapel people suffered, is that the chapel had to be enlarged within approximately twenty years of its opening as the congregation grew so quickly. Did you know, Captain, that this old chapel has been enlarged twice, or more correctly, extended twice? The land didn't permit for it to be widened, and for that reason its length is completely disproportionate to its width."

"Well, no, but you must remember that Shon Gruffydd and yourself have a great advantage over me. I've spent years travelling the world until these last few years. Where was that Nonconformist you mentioned – the master of *Henblas* – when more land was needed to extend the chapel? It's obvious that there's plenty of land behind the chapel. How come they didn't buy more, instead of extending the chapel like an old stocking as it is now?"

"Well, once again", said Sam Puw, "this wasn't down to a lack of taste or a lack of finances either. I heard that the old people offered a good price for some land behind the chapel to extend the house and the chapel. But the original owner's nephew refused to sell even a yard, despite having inherited his uncle's estate with no costs whatsoever. It seems that his wife's family had legal dealings with some Nonconformist from the Caerefron area, and lost the case, and there was nothing to do but demand a pound of flesh. It's no wonder that the old father Huw Llwyd said at a trustee meeting at that time: 'It's a shame that there's no law to enforce the sale of land for a reasonable price when the health and wellbeing of good people is concerned.' Some, you see, call themselves Nonconformists, but after becoming landowners have shown a most unworthy spirit," Sam Puw added.

"Dear me", said Shon Gruffydd "I don't understand how any Nonconformist can refuse to sell land on which to build a House for the Lord. I would have thought they'd be willing to give land free of charge for such a worthy aim."

The reader will note that the chapel I intend to talk about had served one generation before the days of Sam Puw and his companions. The simple building stands on the outskirts of a not un-remarkable village, where many men of distinction were raised, some prominent leaders in notable fields in the church and wider world. The chapel was built early in the last century. As already noted from Sam Puw's comment, the chapel had been extended twice until its length was completely dispro-portionate to its width. But if the chapel was narrow out of necessity, there was broadness, through grace, in the characters of its congregants. The congregation was made up of almost all classes of people. And even though the chapel was outside the village, it was of equal distance between the mountain and the ocean. I can see it this minute in my mind's eye. There it stands with its side to the road, or more correctly, facing the road. It was whitewashed annually before the Great Meeting free of charge by the friends of the cause. The door was at the centre with a window on each side. After entering one could see that at least four square yards of the floor was stone on which stood some half a dozen benches. On the left stands the great pew and the pulpit. Opposite the door, against the wall, were two pews, and most of the pews on the left where on a gradually sloping angle coming to within almost a yard of the ceiling. The pulpit was also built as close to Heaven as possible. The old fathers believed in elevat-ing the preacher as high as they could, and the natural height of the pulpit was a sign of the sincere respect given to the Ministers of Peace. The more romantically spirited preacher was in danger of losing sight of his sermon because of the glorious view from the pulpit. Through the window on the right one could see Foel y Frân towering majestically towards the heavens. On the left was a vast expanse of ocean with ships big and small navigating the waves. On a fine day the bleating of lambs could be heard, and other times the gentle turtle-dove cooing in the branches of the mighty oak tree at the gable end of the chapel.

Nant y Gro Chapel was also close enough to the sea to occasionally hear the waves crashing furiously against Craig y Cyrn. Today the sweet scent of heather wafted on the breeze from the slopes of the Foel; other times one caught a whiff of the seaweed on the beach.

As the chapel was almost an equal distance from the sea and the mountain it's congregants, as expected, were composed of farmers and seamen. These people knew almost as much about the land as the sea. Many of the villagers owned either a boat or a horse, and were in their element handling fish or tending sheep. The notes of "land and sea," could be heard in their worship, one might be praying heartily comparing life to "a ship at sea" thrown about by the waves, followed by perhaps by a kind-hearted farmer who brought to mind the farm and its duties to help him convey his thoughts; and the hustle and bustle of harvest time and the joyful shout of the farmer carrying sheaves could be heard in his prayer. And if the difference was felt in their prayers, it was also seen in their dress and posture. Indeed, on a hot day you could smell the difference. One might have come straight from the cow shed in his sleeved waistcoat smelling heavily of livestock, and the other straight from the boat in his knitted waistcoat smelling of tar. Despite the difference, anointed friendships were formed. The people came from far and wide, but all came with the dew of prayer on their souls.

Perhaps the image seems un-natural, but an hour's fellowship in Nant y Gro would dispel all falsehood from your mind. They came in all weathers, some walking many miles after a hard day's work. They came as they couldn't do otherwise. But it cost them dearly.

"You're here again tonight," someone said to the old Shon Llwyd.

"Yes, lad", said the old pilgrim, "this old body's getting tired, even in the seiat; but my soul doesn't, mind you. Do you know what, the older I get, the more I become two parts: that is, body and soul. There was a time when I thought I had no body, I was all soul somehow. But this old body's making a claim on my soul now. Sometimes my body's tired of these meetings, even though my soul enjoys them. But fair play to the old corpse, it's still on probation, I'm awaiting 'the adoption, which is the redemption of our body.' But this old corpse will become a full member soon enough, and I will be one again. I can stay young then forever. 'They shall mount up with wings as eagles; they shall run and not be weary.' Yes, yes, great things are awaiting us, through God's grace. I'll come to this small chapel while I can. It was worthwhile the old people building the chapel, even if it was only for my sorts. God's best has been greater than a Baron's worst."

CHAPTER II

THE AUTHORITIES

I don't think I ever heard anybody complain that the pews were small at Nant y Gro. Everybody there had a spacious seat. I know well that as a ten-year-old boy I had to stand on a stool to see over the edge. Strangely, it was a visiting doctor who drew my attention to this fact – that the people of Nant y Gro had unusually long necks. Perhaps this was down to the height of the chapel pews – naturalists use the same theory to explain why some remarkable creatures have such long necks. But I was saying that all the seats were large. This is possibly what accounted for the size of the 'Elders' Pew.' It was exceptionally spacious. You can imagine how large it was when I tell you that this is where the children's meeting was held on a Thursday night. Perhaps this is why the children of the Nant still have a strange longing in their blood for the Elders' Pew, wherever they may be. The Elders' Pew, of course, is where the Elders sat, and to their eternal praise, their places were never empty. I've heard it said that some Chapel officials nowadays never attend the seiat, but there were no such wet fish in Nant y Gro.

Huw Elis was the Chapel's announcer, and Wiliam Bartley, the precentor, had an honorary place in the Elders' Pew. It therefore contained "seven men of good repute." Old Samuel Puw sat in the chair beneath the pulpit and the other chair was kept empty for the minister. He lived in the town, a few miles away, and visited occasionally. Shon Gruffydd and John Cunnah claimed the two corners, the precentor and the announcer sat between them, and the other two sat on each side of the pulpit. One would think that it made no difference where anyone sat, but there was a complete understanding among these seven men that no one was to take another's seat. This was out of custom and habit rather than an active agreement. But great significance was given to this, even from outside the Elders' Pew. This was easily seen by observing the flock as they arrived, because after bowing their heads to ask a blessing on the service, each in turn would glance towards the Elders' Pew to see if everyone was in his customary place. I remember well Shon Gruffydd being ill once for six weeks, and that Gershom Tomos one morning dared to sit in his corner. I might as well say it as it is – nobody received any means of grace at that meeting, even though the minister himself filled the Pulpit that Sabbath.

The Reverend Ifor Jenkins, the Pastor of the church, was an affectionate and good natured man. Once met, he was not easily forgotten. His face was scared with the smallpox he came down with as a lad. His two piercing eyes hid under a balcony of thick eyebrows and a broad forehead. One instantly got the impression that he was a strong, pensive man. He wasn't as agile as most however. A condition he suffered from as a student resulting from a damp bed had shortened the sinew in one of his legs and caused him to walk with a slight limp.

Few people knew of Mr Jenkins outside his pastoral circle as he was of a reserved nature. Perhaps his public talents were not of the sort to bring him popularity, but he was an excellent character, a man of strong convictions who left a profound impression on the flock he cared for. Maybe such a man serves his generation just as much, if not more in the long run, than those who travel the length and breadth of the country drawing huge crowds to hear them. This is for certain, he rightly provided the Word of life to his flock from year to year, and there was nobody more popular at home in his pulpit than him. The biggest compliment to Mr Jenkins's abilities and influence was the members of his church. His stamp was apparent on them. He himself was an ardent Nonconformist, and likewise his flock. The principles of Nonconformity were seared into his soul as a promising young student: and in fact cost him his life's big ambition. This is how it was. He caught the attention of his old teacher at Ll____g Grammar School through his swift mastery of Greek and Latin. The Head Teacher was an old school Oxford man, and he saw in Ifor Jenkins one who could easily win a scholarship at Jesus College, Oxford, and bring prestige to the school as a result. When the teacher suggested this to young Ifor, he was mesmerised by the idea. But back then it was impossible for a young Nonconformist to attend that prestigious institution without betraying his Nonconformity, and when his father told Ifor he would have to attend Church if he were to go to Oxford the young lad began to weep in despair – and said: "Father, I'll never go there." Ifor Jenkins won great honours in his conscience that day, even though he lost an Oxford degree after his name. He remained a lifelong student, and he never neglected visiting the flock he cared for. The old minister's name stood for everything the area held in high regard.

Every other Sabbath, the service at Nant y Gro was held in the afternoon as opposed to the morning. Even though the members numbered more than one hundred, they didn't think it beneath them to submit to such arrangements. It's true that the supporters of the Sunday School in those early days protested against this. They wanted the Sunday School in the afternoon every week, instead of alternating every other with the service and having it in the morning. But, as usual, Samuel Puw's opinion and influence outweighed the opposition. "We must remember," he said "the comfort of others beside ourselves. Those who live in *Cefnogwen* will receive no grace at all if we only think of our rights. And another thing, the old lady from the *Fedw* will get no means of grace if we do away with the afternoon service. And remember also that the strong have a duty to support the weak. The way things are, that's how we received them, my friends, and the cause succeeded, but if the order was changed, heaven knows how things would be."

"Things," was the old man Samuel Puw's big word. The word stood for the best substances of both worlds. In the shop he used the word to denote shoes and leather, and at the seiat the great principles of the Gospel. Everybody knew that old Sam's "things", as they said, were things worth having. The same principal governed the honest old fellow's "things" in the shop and his "things" in the chapel. Indeed, Sam Puw's life was one world, and all his "things" bore the same image. The shoes he sold in his shop were almost as eternal as the Gospel he professed. We were almost tempted to believe that the apostle was referring to shoes of this quality when speaking figuratively about having one's "feet shod with the preparation of the gospel of peace." But anyway, everyone who 'watched their step' liked wearing shoes made by Sam Puw, as they believed they could walk more sure-footed in them. The old man put his character into them before his customer got the chance to put their feet in them. It's a great thing indeed that a man's work upholds the authority of his advice.

In practice, Sam Puw was the "chief elder." No authority was needed behind the appointment. His age, his unfaltering loyalty, and the strength of his personality gave him precedent. Some must be given authority, but Sam Puw grew into it unbeknown to himself. Nature, it's true, was kind to him. He was a strong man in body, mind and character. He was all two yards tall, well built and strong boned with two black, piercing eyes. He didn't have the Captain's ability to laugh heartily, in fact, there was little mischief in his nature. He never broke out into excessive joy or sadness. He must have been extremely strong willed. He was always the same, and even though everybody loved him, nobody could be bold with him. He had a fairly rough voice. I remember well how we would cower as children when the old brother knitted his brows. He very rarely needed to raise his voice at home or in chapel, his presence was enough to dispel all trouble. As well as this, he was exceptionally bright. Perhaps his knowledge was not as broad as Mr. Cunnah's, but he was gifted with extraordinary common sense. He moved so slowly and cautiously that he very rarely made a mistake. He seemed so equally capable in everything that it's difficult to ascertain in what field he excelled. He was recognised in

the area as a strong character and as a man who dared
to stand by his principles come what may. His presence
at the seiat was a tower of strength, and indeed, the
seiat is where his strength was felt. As he himself said
"I owe everything to the seiat. I don't know how people can live without means of grace. Only God knows
what I'd be without it. I know that the devil lost a bold
servant when I was won by the love of Jesus Christ. I
often fear the devil, but do you know what, after a seiat
like this one I feel I could lift the *Foel* off its heels. Elijah walked for forty days and forty nights after God's
angel fed him. That's how I see the seiat – as an opportunity to be fed by God."

Everybody looked up to Sam Puw apart from the
man of *Cae Hob*. "I don't know what's got into people," he'd say, "Sam Puw the cobbler only needs to
say something and everybody takes his word for it."
That's true of course, but remember, Sam Puw didn't
lord it over anyone. There was no hint of authority
in his words, but somehow he took everybody with
him, as nobody could see a better path than the one
he suggested. The man of *Cae Hob* had nothing to say
to Sam Puw as there was animosity between his eldest
daughter and Willie, Sam Puw's son. The family of *Cae
Hob* had allowed prejudice to grow between them and
poor Sam Puw as a result of the children's quarrels. An
elder is expected to carry his family on his back and is
held responsible for his children. Indeed, the elder's
wife, no more than the minister's wife, can dress as
she pleases, and if their children happen to be mischievous, their father's position is waved in front of them
so much that some children hate being an Elder's son.
Remember, Sam Puw's children were fairly normal

children, there was nobody more faithful than them in chapel, but their behaviour was more strictly judged due to their father's position.

The family who ran the cobbler's shop were extremely good natured. Their door was always open, and there was no kinder woman in the district than Betsan Puw. The preachers headed there from far and wide. In the shop's parlour to this day there is an old oak trestle chair known as the "preachers" chair. The denomination's chief preachers had sat here, and if all else failed, I think the family would keep hold of the chair despite everything. And what a surprise, for the old chair had a sacred history – it was the chair of Betsan Puw's godly father. "What are these spots on the seat," I asked her once. "Ah my boy," she said, "they're the tear stains of my old godly father. This is where he'd kneel to say the family devotions. He commended us children by name to the Lord, and many a time I saw his sparkling tears run down his cheeks and fall onto the old oak chair. The old chair is worth my father's prayers to me."

"Tears framed in oak," I said to myself listening to her. "I never find Sam Puw so eloquent as when he's in my father's old oak chair" – Betsan Puw added.

Perhaps the old brother's chief distinction was his prayers, and I think this is where his strength lay. Many were more talented than him, he wasn't fiery or articulate when on his knees, but a deep, silent influence swept over everybody when he was wrestling with God. The family of *Llwydiarth Ganol* believed that Sam Puw's prayer could change the weather – they knew for certain that the old man's prayer had saved one of their children when the doctor had given up. The sailors felt when beginning their voyages that they would get "fair wind" if they also got Sam Puw's prayers. Nobody believed that more firmly than Captain Wiliams, captain of the "Angharad", and if you asked him about the foundations of his belief, he would probably tell you the story I will try to repeat in the following chapter.

CHAPTER III

TROUBLES

I was mentioning, wasn't I, why Captain Wiliams believed that Sam Puw's prayers were so effective.

But before telling that story I should say that the Captain, even though he wasn't a chapel official, had a good measure of healthy influence on the spiritual life of the congregation and on the circle of officials. From time to time, many attempts had been made to give him a position, but the Captain always refused, apart from being the Treasurer of the Foreign Mission. "I believe," he said to Mr Jenkins the minister, "that I can be of better service as I am. I don't know why on earth some people want a position. Take the man who lives at *Bryniau Bach*, he's desperate to be an Elder, but I don't want to be a pin cushion for everyone. And apart from that, I can support the excellent brothers who have roles to fulfil much better this way." Yes, the Captain was a pleasant, gracious brother and always had a smile on his face. Strangely, the Captain could say whatever he wanted and nobody was ever offended. Sam Puw and the other Elders had done well by him many a time. Very rarely was anything done without consulting the Captain. As a ship's master he was well versed in the ways of men, and because he had seen a large part of the world and had been among people of all kinds, he had gained a wider experience than most. After leaving the sea his heart became set on the chapel. He went, of course, for summer trips in one of his boats; he liked, as he said, "to taste the salt now and then." But to get to the story, it appears that the Captain had once taken Sam Puw to Dublin in his ship, the "Angharad". On the way back they ran into trouble that could well have been the end of them both.

Shortly after returning, Sam Puw was called to Caerefron on important business, and as he was unable to get back in time for the seiat, the Captain had a wonderful opportunity to tell the story of their strange escape.

Captain Wiliams opened the seiat by reading the passage from the Book of Acts about the Apostle Paul being shipwrecked, and his misfortunes in a rip tide. The Captain explained this "meeting of the seas" near the islands of Crete and Malta.

"Now tell me," he said suddenly, "do you think that the angels know less about the tides of Cardigan Bay than the currents of the Mediterranean? You will never believe the trouble Sam Puw and I had towards Bardsey Island. Do you know what - if the Lord sent his angel then, to save the lives of poor wretched souls on account of the Apostle Paul, he most definitely sent an angel to save us because of Sam Puw. Can I tell you the story?

Well, we were going happily in full sail, and the 'Angharad' was slicing through the waves like a steamer, but suddenly the wind dropped and the old ship was taken by the current towards Bardsey Island. And that's where we were for a few hours dragged back and forth on the various currents. There wasn't a breath of wind, you see, and there was nothing to do but wait for a catastrophe. I didn't give myself or the ship a second thought. I was thinking of Sam Puw. What would the people of Nant y Gro say if he drowned in my care? We were near a place called Hell's Mouth – what a strange place to take an Elder, but I tell you this – I knew Sam Puw would get to heaven and defy the jaws of hell. Every minute I was expecting to see the old ship being hurled against the rocks. Two or three times she was actually within a few yards. Well, there was nothing to do but get into the lifeboat and let the old ship take its chance. You should have seen Sam Puw's face when I told him to get into the boat. And that's where we were for a while, watching the poor old ship rushing to and fro in great tribulation. At long last, Sam Puw got down on his knees in the boat and offered up one of the most intense prayers I've ever heard. And, mark my words, explain things how you like, but the breeze picked up and the sails of the old ship began to billow, and she started defying the tide like a man fully awake. But this is the strange thing, and it's as true as I'm standing in front of you this very minute, the 'Angharad' headed straight towards us like a bear who had found her cubs. She could easily have turned her nose to the sea, never to be seen again. Now, who do think was at the helm? I know there was nobody on board but Jack the dog. Why do you think the old ship came straight towards us as if she had sense? I know who sent the wind, and I'm sure that the angel of the Lord was at the helm of the 'Angharad' that day, I'm certain of it. Do you know what? The angels are good seamen, and who was more worthy of help than Sam Puw. Well, I'll tell you this, it was Sam Puw's prayer that saved us."

It would be very easy to chronicle many similar events that embElished Sam Puw's life, but this is

enough to give you an idea of the man's character, and
to show why he was loved and respected by the friends
of Nant y Gro as a steadfast man of prayer.

Another giant of the Elders' Pew was John Cunnah. He was a bachelor, and around middle aged when
I met him first. He was lodging at the time with Mr.
Hedge – a very useful man who came to the area from
Cornwall. When Mr. Hedge first came to the neighbourhood he couldn't speak a word of Welsh. He
used to pray in English, and even though the majority
of the old saints couldn't understand him, they half-
hoped that the Good Lord understood that language.
Huw Elis occasionally ventured an 'Amen,' sometimes
even saying the word in the right place. But in time Mr.
Hedge came to speak broken Welsh and was of great
service to the cause.

Mr Cunnah was the village schoolmaster, and was
known by the children as the "old school." He was a
small and very exact man. He had an authoritative, me-
tallic voice; and I would have thought that, by nature,
there was no more warmth in him than in the mul-
tiplication table. He did everything according to the
'rule of three.' It was he who looked after the chapel
accounts. It would do some people good to look at his
old books – they are still available, and the calculations
in them written in the neatest copperplate.

I remember asking my mother once: "How come
Mr. Cunnah didn't get married, mam?" And as soon as
I asked the question some kind of melancholy spread
over her face, and she started to explain the problem
I hadn't been able to solve. She said that Mr Cunnah,
shortly after coming to the area, fell in love with Miss

Jenkins, one of the fairest maidens in the Nant. Her mother and father, Joseph and Gwen Jenkins, *Y Tyddyn*, were very responsible people and were prominent members at Nant y Gro. Mr. Cunnah was not a chapel member when he first arrived. He did go to church, or chapel occasionally, but when he started spending time with the only daughter of Joseph and Gwen Jenkins, she influenced him spiritually. In fact, she would have nothing to do with him unless he became a member of the chapel. In time, he eventually gave in. That Thursday night in 18— when he first attended the seiat will be long remembered. It was the talking point of the village for days. Eventually they decided to get married, a date was appointed and everyone was interested in the occasion. The wedding day arrived; everything was ready. The entire village came to celebrate the event as the two of them were fairly well known. Two white horses were seen pulling a 'closed carriage' to the *Tyddyn*, and shortly afterwards Miss Jenkins came out in a white dress. My mother always said she was a pretty girl, but that day she looked like an angel. There were flags waving everywhere, and people shouting their good wishes, and when the carriage began to leave, someone fired a gunshot to add to the merriment. But that startled the horses. They galloped down the hill, and to everyone's horror they sped through the village and past the church until the carriage crashed into Barron Owain's cenotaph. The carriage was smashed to smithereens, many were injured, and Miss Jenkins was thrown out and killed instantly.

My mother was unable to continue with the story. But more than once after that I heard people say that the sad occasion had left a deep impression on Mr

Cunnah's mind. For weeks on end he wrestled with his own thoughts, troubled by doubts; he was unable to see why his heart's most beautiful desires and his life's most refined hopes had been shattered. I heard that Sam Puw had been especially loyal to him. He tried to keep Mr Cunnah's mind on the things that Miss Jenkins held so dear. Mr. Cunnah continued to love Jenny after losing her. He drank from the well of memories and his thirst was quenched. The life to which his beloved had gone became to him a glorious reality, and in that hope he became a most excellent man. The echoes of this event was heard in all his counsels. I remember one very good seiat where Mr. Cunnah happened to be leading. He opened the fellowship by pointing out how similar events affect people differently according to their state of mind. He explained this by referring to the stories of Pharo and Job, - how painful situations inspired rebellion in one but humility in the other.

"Where I grew up," he said, "there lived a small farmer. He had two or three fields on a ragged hillside with very shallow soil, and the rest of his fields in a fertile valley. The old farmer was always confused as to how to ask God to bless his farm. 'If I ask for plenty of sunshine for the wet fields in the valley,' he said, 'then the dry fields on the hillside will burn.' His farm wasn't very big," said Mr. Cunnah, "but it was obvious that he should have at least two suns to farm it purposefully." Before Mr. Cunnah had the opportunity to apply his message, Mari Llwyd was on her feet.

"Do you know what, Mr Cunnah. I have a lot of sympathy towards that farmer. Brothers and sisters, I have, as you know, two lads at sea, and when they're sailing in opposite directions it's impossible to know how to pray that both get fair wind. I think there should be two winds, at least. What do you think, Mr. Cunnah?"

"Well, dear sister," said Mr. Cunnah, "if you had two winds, and that farmer I mentioned had two suns, somebody would no doubt want three. That will never do."

"Well, well," said the old woman, "what can we do but make the best of the worst."

"But," said Mr. Cunnah, taking up the subject once more. "I wasn't referring to the farmer, but to his fields – I wanted to show you how the same sun greens one field but scorches the other, because there's a difference in the soil. The Great Lord in his Providence smiles on some people, and as they progress in life their hearts get proud and they forget God, whilst others succeed and glorify God. The storms of life don't affect everybody the same – some harden under the treatment, whilst others submit under God's mighty hand." Mr Cunnah bowed his head, a tear ran down his cheek and a quiver came to his voice.

"I too," he said, "found myself in circumstances where I felt my heart rising up in rebellion. Had I listened to those impulses back then, I wouldn't be here tonight. But through the help of God's grace, and the generous assistance of this dear brother," and he gestured to Sam Puw, "I was given grace to submit, and the storm drove me closer to the Lord. Yes, yes, cross winds have their stories in our lives, don't they just."

Mr. Cunnah became a very useful man to the cause, and earned great trust in the area. As he was a good scholar, and many were unable to write back then, everyone came to him for a favour. When there was a misunderstanding between a farmer and a land-owner, he was always the advocate. The area was heavily indebted to him. He served everybody willingly, and helped many people out of all kinds of trouble. When Bob, Maria Jones's son, was caught poaching, and ordered to pay a heavy fine or else face imprisonment, Mr. Cunnah paid the amount due. When Miss Huws, *Y Fron*, was left without mother or father, Mr Cunnah proved to be a faithful benefactor. Miss Huws was an excellent girl, and fought hard to keep the old family home for herself, her brothers and her sisters. Shortly after burying her father she received a letter from a solicitor asking her to pay the mortgage of £500 on the farm. Everyone believed that this was nothing but a mean attempt to strip the orphaned children of their home in order to secure the farm for somebody else. Mr Cunnah's tireless labour saved the day. Indeed, he touched everyone's life in the village and the surrounding area. He kept a night school during the winter months and many of the lads at sea came to him for lessons. Many are indebted to him for the responsible positions which they hold today.

CHAPTER IV

A STONEMASON, A SHEPHERD
AND A SAILOR

Before leaving the Elders' Pew, I would like to say a few words about the other three elders I mentioned - Shon Gruffydd the Stonemason, Gershom Tomos the Shepherd and Anthony Jones the Sailor. One could hardly imagine three so different.

Shon Gruffydd was an amicable old man. He was the church's "dear disciple", and was known amongst ourselves as the "old Jeremiah," though there was more admiration than insult in the name, mind you. He was a stone mason and gravestone inscriber by trade. I never understood what compelled such a warm hearted man to work with such cold stones. But even though he was a working man by trade, he was made a gentleman by nature. A more charming personality was difficult to come by. He didn't have Sam Puw's strength, nor John Cunnah's ability, but he had a gentleness about him that won everyone's affection.

He was always clean and well-dressed, and his long, white, flowing beard gave him a somewhat patriarchal appearance. Shon Gruffydd and his wife were well-known for their cleanliness. They lived in a small thatched roof cottage that was as neat as ninepence. The well maintained garden at the front of the house drew everyone's attention. Two holly trees grew either side of the door and a box hedge enclosed the garden.

I remember how Shon Gruffydd shaped the hedge at each end of the gate to resemble two cockerels. He carried pebbles to make a pretty path from the gate to the door, and white shells from the seaside to form a border.

The children of the chapel had one chief ambition – to have tea with Shon Gruffydd, and every one of us went in turn. The small cottage was exceptionally cosy, especially under the large chimney which was a kitchen in itself. I can see Shon Gruffydd this minute sitting in his oak chair, which had been scrubbed as clean as Nelw Gruffydd's tireless arm could get it. The round table was only covered with a tablecloth on Sunday, but was subject to the scrubbing brush on a daily basis. Opposite the oak chair was an old fashioned settle. As a rule, that's where Nelw sat diligently knitting stockings. Many a time I sat on the three legged stool warming my feet by the peat fire. And what tea Nelw Gruffydd made! I can still taste the cheese and the griddle bread.

Even though Shon Gruffydd was not a great thinker, he avidly read his denomination's periodicals. His main books however where the Bible, *Pilgrim's Progress* [2] and *The Book of the Three Birds.* [3] "Shon Gruffydd understands things with his heart", Captain Wiliams once said. "His heart, like the two disciples on the road to Emmaus, would have recognised the Saviour a long time before his head could." It must be said he could explain Bible verses with Mathew Henry's capacity, but he did that not through intellect but through an unerr-

2   The Welsh translation being 'Taith y Pererin'

3   In Welsh 'Llyfr y Tri Aderyn' – A book written by the Welsh Puritan Mystic, Morgan Llwyd in 1685.

ing spiritual instinct. Heaven most definitely bestowed him her secrets. He accomplished his work as an elder with unending dedication. He visited the sick and neglectful, he walked from house to house encouraging faithfulness, but refrained from "evil gossip." His presence was like sunshine in May, and his prayers like dewdrops on flowers. I never remember seeing him without a smile on his face. I saw him weeping many a time, but the rainbow would brighten his tears, and the tears would brighten his vision.

Seeing him listening to the Gospel was a means of grace. His enthusiasm was contagious. When the preacher happened to make a striking remark, the old man was unable to contain his enjoyment; he nodded at Sam Puw who sat in the chair next to him, he cast his eyes with a wonderful smile at Mr. Cunnah, and gave Huw Elis a nudge until the Elders' Pew was buzzing. He charged the congregation with his "Amens" and "Yes, Yesses". It's no wonder that Captain Wiliams said "I don't even have to thank a man for preaching if those in the Elders' Pew at Nant y Gro have listened to him."

Strangely, it was the dignity and greatness of Christ and not the cross and the crown of thorns that fascinated Shon Gruffydd more than anything else. You would think that the cross and the sufferings of Christ would have the greatest appeal to him, but the victory of Christ, his glorious resurrection and his ascension to the right hand of God was his favourite topic. Some can't preach a good sermon without mentioning a death bed and a cemetery; but the empty tomb and the living Christ got Shon Gruffydd's main attention.

I remember well one inspiring service. The sermon was on "*Who is this that cometh from Edom, with red garments from Bozrah? He is glorious in his apparel, and walketh in his great strength?*" Everyone saw that the theme had struck the tenderest chord in the old brother, because before the preacher had time to read the verse, Shon Gruffydd took it from his lips. The preacher was describing Christ during those three strange nights where he had been in the tomb, having gone to Hades to fight with the unicorns and dragons of hell, - he trampled his enemies before him, he shattered the chains, the tale-bearers of hell fled, and, despite the stone and the watchmen, behold the chief warrior of Bozra, rising on the third day having conquered death and the grave. If you could hear the old brother's 'Amens'! The sparks flew from his soul charging everyone. Before long the preacher exuberantly repeated the words and emphasised "travelling in the greatness of his strength," and he shouted at the top of his voice "It wasn't some half-hearted feat with our Saviour," "No, never" said the old elder equally as loud. "No," said the preacher, "he had plenty in reserve – in the greatness of his strength." "Glory to Him", said Shon Gruffydd, "we'll come up in his shadow." The place was alive with the divine fire. The preacher tried to explain the truths by means of hymns, but Shon Gruffydd took them from his mouth. Yes, the old warrior spent his life with the living Christ; this is without doubt what counted for his hopeful spirit. I've heard it said that, when carving names on headstones, he would break out in ecstasy in the lonely cemetery.

Even though Shon Gruffydd was an affectionate and sensitive man by nature, losing his only child had

no doubt softened him. He and Nelw Gruffydd doted on Gwen. Sam Puw called one of his own children
by the same name in memory of her. Little Gwen
died of tuberculosis – the area's old enemy. She was
a very old fashioned child. She insisted on getting up
one morning to plant *Sweet Wiliam* "so you can have
something to remember me," she said "when I've
gone to plant flowers with Jesus." And the flowers
were known as Gwen's flowers among the children of
the area ever since.

When she was very ill one morning, she asked her
mother: "Do you think the river of death is very *deep*,
mam?" Nelw Gruffydd tried to avoid the question by
focusing on something else. But Gwen asked a second
time: "Do you think the river of death is over my *head*,
mam? How does that verse go? Oh yes, 'On the shores
of Jordan *deep*," said Gwen, emphasising the last word.
"Is the water over my head, mam?"

The distraught mother wasn't sure how to answer,
and as she hesitated, she saw Gwen's eyes welling up,
and she asked exuberantly "Is the water over Jesus's
head, then mam?" "Oh, no my child" said Nelw Gruffydd through her tears. "I know that Jesus Christ has
crossed it for sure." "All right", said little Gwen, with a
victorious heavenly smile on her lips. "I'll ask Him to
take me in his arms," and she crossed the river singing:

"A friend is he in the river of death
Who keeps my head above the wave" [4]

The incident left a very deep impression on Shon

---

4   *A translation of the first two lines of a well-known hymn
composed by the Welsh hymn writer Evan Evans, known by his
bardic name of Ieuan Glan Geirionydd.*

Gruffydd, but he couldn't bear Ieuan Glan Geiriony-dd's old hymn after that, and he was vehemently opposed to teaching children about the depth of the Jordan.

The two other elders – Gershom Tomos, the shepherd of *Hafod y Cwm*, and Anthony Jones, the old sailor, had many virtues, but there was no comparison between them and the other three. The shepherd was an innocent enough man, but there was something rather obstinate about Anthony Jones. He was always wronged by someone or other. He was extremely annoyed one time when he was appointed to pray on Thanksgiving morning, where he and his wife thought that he should have been appointed for the evening service. He complained that everybody was against him. "It doesn't matter what I propose, it's never accepted." This was his constant tirade. He thought that everyone was against him, but in reality, he was at odds with everybody else – except his wife, in whom he had a ready supporter. Poor thing, he could think of an amendment to every proposal, and he would be sure to say "This is what they do in such and such a place". But nothing availed. Of course, he was given every fair play, but somehow everything withered under his hands. He caused a lot of anguish to the other elders, but as Captain Wiliams said, "it's good for us to have an old whinger like Anth'ny, or Heaven would be no change at all.

'All the brothers will be there as one
With nobody at odds,'

But remember that Nant y Gro is on earth, even though it's easy to forget that sometimes in certain company."

What accounted for Anthony Jones' weakness, I wonder? It must be said he was extremely faithful in all services, and no one could fault his way of life. However, everyone though he was fond of money. That was certainly the root of his objection to the Foreign Mission. As a sailor, he had seen his fair share of the world. One time he said "I am not going to give my money to keep those missionaries living like noblemen, that's for sure." He tried to corrupt people's minds against the missionaries, and in every age, one doesn't need much genius to persuade some people from not parting with their money. But luckily for this important cause, Captain Wiliams, who had seen more of the world than him, and much more of the life and work of the missionaries, was a fervent supporter of the Mission.

Another reason for Anthony Jones' unpopularity was his constant habit of blaming his fellow elders. Somehow, people don't think much of a man who criticizes a group of people when he chooses to remain within that group himself. "I don't know how to account for the fact", said Anthony Jones once to Captain Wiliams. "but everyone in this chapel comes to me with their complaints, and remember this, Captain, there are a lot of complaints against the elders, you don't hear half the things people say." "Well no, thank God," said the Captain "they wouldn't dare say much to me about the elders, even though I'm not an elder myself. But you remember, Anthony, people don't come to you with their complaints because they respect you, it's because they don't respect you. They know, you see, that you're not loyal to your brothers.

You think about it this way - Mr. Perkins, the agent, comes to your house at election time to ask for your vote, but there's no chance he'd go to Sam Puw. Why, do you think? You're both elders in the same chapel! It's easy enough for you and your wife to boast that the agent called, but remember that people guess your character through the agent's visit. Remember, Anthony, there are some people on this earth who can't be bought with a bribe! Now, you let people believe that you're loyal to your brothers and you'll get less of their complaints. It's miserable work being a scavenger in God's church. Complain less, dear Anth'ny and work more. I often think of what the old man, my father, used to say, 'that there are six tendons from a man's brain to his eyes, eight to his ear, but only three to his tongue, and that a man should hear and see twice as much as he says.' It would do us a lot of good to remember that."

When given the chance, Anthony Jones and his wife were also fond of talking about their money. They boasted that they had as much means as anybody in the Nant, but neither of them could bear any mention of money in the chapel. The noise of the offering set their teeth on edge. Everyone knew why.

When Anthony Jones retired from the sea, he started selling coal – "just so Anthony could have something to do," as Mrs Jones said. But even though Anthony Jones and his wife claimed to have plenty of money whenever the occasion lent itself, they never missed the chance to taunt "we wouldn't have a single crust if everyone was like the chapel people. Things would be pretty bleak for us selling coal if it weren't for the people of the Church, and Anthony and I often talk of going to Church altogether." That was the old brother's weakness, he took his business to chapel, and the chapel (notice, not his religion) to his business. The coal gave its colour to everything, but it contained more colour than heat. Anthony Jones and his wife were never happy without complaining and threatening going to Church. "But," as the old Captain said. He was the chapel's freelance – "there's no danger that Anthony will ever go to the Church. He's too fond of his place in the Elders' Pew. However he got into it, you could never get him out of it. Do you know what, it's harder to convince a miser than a drunkard. I've never seen such a thing, you would turn a man out for getting drunk, but a man can be an elder even if he's the greatest miser, even though the Bible sets them both on the same level." There was a lot of truth, no doubt, in what the Captain said, but Anthony Jones was too cunning for anyone apart from the world to catch. Avarice was the blemish on Anthony Jones' life. If he was as generous with his money as he was with his advice he would have made a great Christian.

Gersham Tomos, yr Hafod, the other Elder mentioned, was a man void of both fault and excellence. I wouldn't be surprised if he had fallen under Anthony Jones' paws – that was his main weakness. The shepherd however, was blessed with a virtuous wife and she kept him within limits. She must have been a genius with money as she managed to raise a houseful of children on eight shillings a week. They walked the three mile journey from the Hafod to the chapel in all weathers, and as a rule, were the first to arrive. Over his life, he walked miles to the chapel. Captain Wiliams calculated that he must have walked the circumference of the earth. As he returned home from the seiat one winter's night, a terrible storm broke out. The snow had fallen for two days prior to this. They tried to persuade the shepherd to stay in the village that evening, but despite all incitements he adamantly started home. "I know the paths like the back of my hand," he said "and besides, the wife will be waiting for me." That night, as usual, the shepherd's wife set a candle in the window to cast its weakly light on her husband's path. The wind howled and threw the snow with ravaging force into the shepherd's face. His wife sat down and waited hours for him. When she dared to open the door to try and hear her husband's footsteps in the yard, the wind threw the snow until it almost filled the house. There was nothing to do but sit and wait. Dawn broke, but the shepherd had still not arrived. Very early that day the wife hurried to the village to enquire about him. She was assured that he had insisted on setting home, despite everyone's pleas. The entire village set out to search, and they found that the storm had left the Hafod's wife a widow, and seven children fatherless. The old shepherd's body was found under a carpet of snow in the posture of one praying.

CHAPTER V

The Chapel House Family

The Chapel House was a very interesting place indeed. That's where many of the saints gathered for discussions before and after the Sunday and weeknight services.

I'm unsure whether heaven has a place in calling or electing people to live in a Chapel House, but I could easily imagine that Wiliam and Catrin Elis filled the "calling" as they were so competent in this important role. I wholeheartedly believe that exceptional talent is needed, especially the gift of wisdom and patience, to do this job effectively. Catrin Elis, however, was part of the "succession" – her family were in the Chapel House before her. But Wiliam Elis was like Melchizedek, with neither mother nor father in the post.

"I vaguely remember Catrin's grandfather keeping the Chapel House," said Sam Puw when conversing in the Chapel House one evening. "Do you know," he said "things have changed quite a lot since then. Her grandfather was the bell-ringer and lived in the Chapel House as well."

"Good gracious," said Shon Gruffydd, "how on an earth could he do both jobs? We'd never put up with such a thing nowadays."

"Perhaps," said the Captain mischievously, "he was fulfilling that verse from Scripture – how does it go,

Sam Puw – 'Serving God and Mammon?'"

"Well, no, fair play, the old bell ringer was a very good man; but as you know things weren't the same back then. In those days the old people started the service before Church, and then a great crowd of them would head off to Church for the 'service' after having the 'sermon' in chapel. A service and a sermon were two different things for them, see, - that's probably what's behind the old saying – 'he reads like a parson;' you never hear anyone saying 'he preaches like a Parson."

"I've heard it said," said Shon Gruffydd "that the old bell-ringer was more of a chapel man than a churchgoer after he was saved."

"How does that story go about him digging a grave for one of the old saints here in Nant y Gro, Sam Puw?" said the Captain.

"Oh yes. Well, I'll tell you: the old bell ringer was instructed to dig a grave for an old Christian of this chapel *behind the church.* I would have thought that the cemetery was pretty wet down that end, and as the old brother opened the grave it was filling with water. He went to see the parson to complain, that it wasn't fit to bury anyone there. 'Good heavens,' said the Parson, 'what's a little bit of water? Have you ever heard of a burial at sea?' 'Oh yes,' said the old bell-ringer, 'but I never heard of anyone *digging* a grave there.'

"Fair play to the old bell ringer," said the Captain. "He must have been quite a chapel man, mustn't he."

"Somebody complained to him once," said Sam Puw, "that he didn't bury everyone the same. I have no idea what they meant, but this is how the old bell ringer replied: 'Did you ever hear of anybody rising again after I buried them?' No, he buried everyone in the spirit of the service with 'true hope of certainty.' The old brother got tired of burying and bell-ringing, and he was known as 'The Chapel House Man' at the end of his life."

"Do you know what," said Sam Puw, pushing his spectacles from his eyes up onto his forehead and crossing one leg over the other, "things have changed quite a lot during my time. If this world hasn't got better then it's altered significantly. Just think! They would deal with chapel matters in the parlour in the Crown back then. Of course, the family who ran the Crown were respectable members of the Nant, and were very fond of driving the preachers around, and one room is the Crown was known as 'the Elders' parlour.' You'd never put up with such a thing now."

"Well, yes, but remember," said Mr. Cunnah, "people didn't look at a glass of beer the same back then."

"Oh, good heavens, no," said Sam Puw. "I remember the time when every notable farmer in this area brewed at home; beer and religion were friends back then. That's why, I think, a church and a tavern were built next to each other. But the old people where just as honest as us, remember. They just didn't see things in the same light."

"It was night, wasn't it, Sam Puw," said the Captain, vigorously drawing smoke through his pipe.

"Well, perhaps 'night' would be better," said Sam Puw slowly, "but I think within another fifty years, Captain, people will view smoking as we view drinking.

What sense is there living in smoke like there's here to-night when we passed last night to pay though our noses to stop the Chapel House chimney from smoking."

"Hang on, Sam Puw, point of order; you're going off the subject now. We were talking about drinking, weren't we?" said the Captain.

"Well, hold on one minute," said Mr. Cunnah, "we had gone off topic long before talking about drink. We were talking about the Chapel House."

"Yes, yes," said Sam Puw, "but that's what I was going to say, that this Chapel House in its present form was one of the first fruits of the temperance revival. When the temperance revival broke out, see, that's when they left the Crown's parlour and decided to enlarge the Chapel House, on the condition that the Elders could use this room. There was only a kitchen and bed-chamber in the old house, and because there was little room to extend the house, they decided to build upwards.

"Fair play to the old people," said the Captain. "They were wise enough to understand if the squire owned the ground, the Lord owned the sky. How would you appropriate that verse, Sam Puw, "The earth is the Lord's, and all that therein is" with the fact that there wasn't enough room to build a Chapel House?

"And now you're trying to lead me off topic again," said Sam Puw.

Many a night were spent in such pleasant conversations in the dear old Chapel House. Remember that much more serious matters were dealt with when needed. The 'Five Points of Calvinism' and the like were intellectually debated in turn.

As a child I was extremely jealous of Chapel House children because of their privileges. When on rainy, stormy night we had to walk great distances over muddy roads and remote footpaths, they could run to chapel without even getting their feet wet. And another thing, the people of Nant y Gro sometimes brought generous gifts to the Chapel House children. One would bring an apple, another plumbs, and they got sweets from the people who kept the shop. Many a time I told my mother that I wish I had been born in the Chapel House. The local farmers were also fairly generous with the Chapel House family. One would bring butter, another eggs and they would get enough potatoes to see them through winter. Of course, in return Catrin Elis lent them an umbrella, or a shawl, or a large coat when needed, and the Chapel House on a seiat evening was more like a Left Luggage Office than anything else. This is how the conversation went every Thursday night, "Can I leave this basket here whilst I'm in chapel, Catrin Elis?" Thursday night, the seiat evening at Nant y Gro, was the busiest night for the village traders. The local farmers conducted the business of both worlds that evening, and as a result the Chapel House was used unsparingly. The women brought their baskets there full of eggs and butter, and after the seiat they took them to the shops to exchange for tea, sugar and the like.

And whilst the mothers would be in the shops, their sons, after the seiat, would gather around the village pump in summer. But if it was wet they would head off to the smithy. Scores of times I heard my mother ask "Can the children stay in the Chapel House whilst I nip to the shop?" The Chapel House would be full of children from the neighbouring farms, and it would be inappropriate to mention the mess made there sometimes. Somehow everyone felt they had a claim on the Chapel House apart from Wiliam and Catrin Elis. It amazes me to think how patient they were at times like these.

Wiliam Elis, the Chapel House, was a quiet man, and like he said "Catrin here can speak enough for both of us." Both he and his wife had one obvious virtue. No gossip ever left the Chapel House. The conversations there were treated as sacredly confidential, and that proved a great benefit to the cause. Catrin Elis was taught by her family to 'hold her tongue,' as she said, and remember, that's quite an accomplishment for a woman, and especially for Catrin Elis who was naturally talkative and of a fairly fiery temperament. But even though the wife of the Chapel House was talkative, she could keep a secret, and as everyone knew that, she heard plenty of them. Almost everyone in Nant y Gro was related to each other, and if the wife of the Chapel House suggested what Jane said about her cousin Mari, well – all hell would break loose. Catrin Elis learnt when to hold her tongue. The only one who would deeply disturb the old sister was Anthony Jones. As Catrin Elis said, "I don't have any ill-feeling towards Anthony, you know. If only he spoke as a man instead of throwing jibes and making suggestions. If you think of Sam Puw, he says some pretty mean things sometimes, but you know, he says things so honestly and unmaliciously that you can't be angry with him. And another thing, when Sam Puw says something, you know what he's saying, and that's the end of it. That's why I get angry with Anthony Jones, you don't know where he finishes. Think about that paraffin bill that caused so much trouble. Our Wiliam wasn't troubled by anything that was said, it was the suggestion in Anthony Jones's word - 'I don't know where this paraffin goes.' The emphasis on the 'I' was the problem, see," said Catrin Elis. "Often it's not what you say that hurts people, but how you say it. Everyone knew where the paraffin went. Wil and I weren't drinking it, but Anthony's words, like his feet, turn in every direction. Like the hands on that clock, you can't tell if its quarter past nine or quarter to three when it's hands are on nine and three, and Anth'ny is pretty much the same."

The Chapel House was frequently used by the preachers too. Catrin Elis kept a pair of stockings for them, and many a preacher, soaked to the bone, felt extremely grateful to the kind old woman for some dry socks to put on. Even though Wiliam Elis was an average sized man, he had one pair of trousers that were made to fit everyone – fat and thin, tall and short. The great problem the friends had was this: How did Mr. Jenkins the Minister, a stout man, get into Wiliam Elis's trousers. But the practical problem one old friend faced was getting himself out of them. However, everyone was good spirited once wearing the clothes of Wiliam Elis, the Chapel House.

Once, when Mr. Jenkins's clothes were drying by the fire, Catrin Elis ran to open the chapel, and who happened to be at the door waiting but Anthony Jones's wife. Catrin Elis said, "Mr Jenkins, poor creature, is soaked through." "Huh", she replied, "he'll be dry enough when he'll get up into that pulpit, I'm sure." The wife of the Chapel House found it very difficult to hold her tongue, as she practically idolized the Minister.

As I grew up I realised that keeping the Chapel House wasn't all a bed of roses. As I mentioned previously, Wiliam Elis was a quiet, tranquil man. He cared for the chapel conscientiously; but of course, sometimes things went wrong. One such mishap was that the oil from one of the lamps leaked into the pew used by Miss Lewis, *y Dyffryn*. As Wiliam Elis said. "I'd prefer it to run into everybody's pew, but what can you do, a man can't arrange accidents, you know. On a cold morning I light two or three of these lamps to warm the place up a bit before people come to chapel. Somehow or other there must have been a crack in the lamp near Miss Lewis's pew. I think Miss Lewis had a new gown on that morning, and she sat in the paraffin – it was awful – but goodness me – she gave me an earful. I tried my best to explain to her, but before I could get a word in the words just flowed like a torrent from her mouth. 'You set about it deliberately', she said 'to get revenge on me, our pew is dirtier than anyone else's. When Miss Wynne and I came here last Sunday I had to wipe the dust off the pew to save her spoiling her new gown. You remember, Wiliam, our clothes cost us something, and you remember, not everybody puts a shilling into the collection like Miss Wynne. Maybe if I didn't pay for my pew, like some people, I'd get more respect and a cleaner pew."

Poor fellow. The man of the Chapel House paid dearly for his house and his honours. As Captain Wiliams said. "Money is the cheapest thing you can give for anything, and remember, the things you get for nothing are the things that cost you most – even your self-respect sometimes. It's much easier to pay for things in cash than in kind. You think about it like this.

Your shilling and mine are worth the same in the market. But you can't pay for a hundred potatoes with a hundred potatoes, because there may be a difference between them. It's the same with butter. You can give a pound of butter for a pound of butter, but there could be difference in the quality. That's why payment in kind is unsatisfactory. I never saw anyone lending a bucketful of coal thinking that someone else's bucketful would be the same. That's the beauty of paying in cash. Money is more honest that the people who deal with it. That's the difference between the sailors and you farmers. I have to pay wages to my sailors; they expect nothing but their wages. But as for the farmhands, they don't know when their wages stop and charity starts. Talk to their master and you'd think that the house, the milk and the potatoes and the like are gifts, and in a way they are, but ask the worker and he'll say that everything is part of his wage. There's no nonsense like that at sea. Never take things for free – that's my policy. I'm worried that Wiliam Elis has to pay very dearly for what he gets."

One very contentious issue was the airing of Nant y Gro Chapel. Mr. Cunnah was all for getting plenty of fresh air into the chapel, and he was supported by Captain Wiliams. It was from the Captain that I heard this saying first – "If you were to put a man in a bottle, some of you wouldn't be happy without corking it too." He said this to the husband and wife of the *Fron* If I remember rightly. The *Fron* family were firmly in favour of shutting every door and window. The first thing the wife of the *Fron* did, after taking her pew, was to glance at the door to see if the key was in the lock, in case she caught a draught through the keyhole. The lady of the *Fron* had probably received many invaluable blessings at Nant y Gro, but people only ever heard her say that she'd had nothing there but a draught.

Between Mr. Cunnah and Captain Wiliams on the one hand, and the *Fron* family and many like-minded individuals on the other, Wiliam Elis found it very difficult. Unfortunately, he and Catrin Elis were prejudiced towards closing every door and window. It must be said that fresh air was not a full member in the Nant, in fact, it was banished from every service. "I'll never come to Chapel, Wiliam Elis, unless you close that door," said the lady of the *Fron*. There was a nice double door on the chapel, but I never remember seeing it fully open. I often wondered in amazement about that, especially when I saw Mr Jenkins, *y Tyddyn*, trying to squeeze through it sideways, and many others too come to think of it – but to fully open the door would be an unforgivable sin.

"Seriously," said Mr. Cunnah to Catrin Elis whilst leaving the service one warm afternoon in June, "Did you see how people were sleeping this afternoon? It was a shame seeing the preacher straining himself trying to keep people awake, and you're to blame as you didn't open the door or one of the windows. Look, Catrin Elis, if you're scared of angering the *Fron* family then open the door fully between the services. I know the windows have been nailed shut."

"Mr Cunnah, dear," said Catrin Elis, "Who knows what an earth would go into the chapel. An old rearing sow wandered in when poor mother was alive, and caused such loss and damage. And even if every animal kept away, the place would be full of dust, and dust is easier to see, Mr. Cunnah, than air, and is much worse for clothes. You men would like to see me with a cloth in my hand from dawn till dusk."

The Gospel must be eternal if it can withstand the prejudices and superstitions of good people. It's funny hearing people sing, "O Lord, send a breeze," when they reject by nature what they desire through grace.

CHAPTER VI

THE PRECENTOR

William Bartley, as you remember, was the name of Nant y Gro's "Precentor", and by virtue of his post he sat in the Great Pew with the dignity of a man who felt his importance. Bartley was an old red-headed man with two uneasy blue eyes. He once had a thick crop of hair but had acquired a bald crown many years ago. He shaved his beard completely so that his mouth was easily able to fulfil its role. He permitted a flurry of hair to grow under his chin to keep his neck cosy. Remember, it wasn't fashion or habit that dictated how many hairs were allowed to grow on his face, but his post. He looked rather strange with a thick mane of hair behind his head, a substantial beard beneath his chin, with a clean shaven face and a bald crown. He was blessed with good health. Indeed, he boasted that he had never drunk a bottle of medicine, or spent a day ill in bed. He had unlimited zeal for his role, and woe betide anyone who dared interfere with his work.

I don't think he missed a single service in the forty years he held the post. In fact, he was so faithful that nobody else got the chance to develop the talent of leading the singing. Perhaps it would have benefited the singing if the old fellow had been ill occasionally, like ordinary mortals, or if he had been broadminded enough to give the younger ones the chance to occasionally practice their talents. As Captain Wiliams said, "being overzealous in your role is almost as much of a drawback to the cause as disloyalty. Some people fill their post so much that they leave them empty. The one who raises successors – that's the man. No one should love his post so much as to place the cause at a disadvantage." The old fellow's virtue almost became a fault. He did himself and the post a disservice by thinking that it was impossible to sing at Nant y Gro without him. You could fault his judgment, but no-body could doubt his intentions.

Wiliam Bartley fulfilled his role of *raising* the song in the fullest sense of the word – it was obvious by his posture that the singing needed quite a bit of bolster-ing. Captain Wiliams knew something about raising an anchor – he had felt its weight a thousand times. We as children knew about raising a pitcher of water from 'Arthur's Well'. I remember clearly, during the summer months, how we had to drop the pitcher to the bot-tom of the well, and the trouble that followed trying to retrieve it. But raising an anchor for the Captain, or raising a pitcher of water for the children, was nothing compared to raising the song for Bartley. What effort!

After the hymn was announced Bartley would put his spectacles on his nose and quickly flick through the pages of the hymnbook, then the book with the music. Finally he scratched his neck and coughed at least three times. He struck the tuning-fork twice on his knee with the skill of a well-practised man, began to hum some-thing, and a noise was heard long before a distinct note was formed. And finally, the precentor rose to his feet as a sign for the audience to follow suit, but the tune started before many of the slower ones were standing.

In his best days Bartley was blessed with a loud,

penetrating voice. He made sure to sing loud enough for at least three of his closest friends. Everyone knew that Sam Puw could only sing two lines of the old hymn "Salvation is like the sea", and did that in his own peculiar way, to the tune called 'The Old Hundredth', so that Bartley expected very little help from him. Shon Gruffydd wasn't too bad at singing in his own time.

It was interesting to hear the old people slurring the notes of some of the old tunes, especially 'Deemster'. You've seen a wagon heavy-laden with coal being hauled up a steep hill; you've heard the sound of the horseshoes, the click of the tresses, the squeak of the wheels and the driver urging on his exhausted horses; that's what was heard during the singing of 'Deemster' – noises, squeaks and shouts. Even though Bartley was the precentor, when 'Deemster' was being sung, not even a wizard could guess who was leading the song – as everyone would start and finish many times over before the tune ended. For a bar or two the man of the *Plas* could be heard roaring in a bass voice with a thunderous boom; then, whilst the man of the *Fron* began to bawl, he would sit down to catch his breath before renewing the attack. Everyone was determined to hear his own voice, and everyone thought they had done an honest day's work before sitting down. However, Bartley always made it safely to the end of the tune if Mari Jones, *Llidiart Uchaf*, was present. I heard that Mari had a melodious voice when she was young, but losing her teeth had greatly affected her voice. She made no attempt whatsoever at saying the words, but she sang with all her might, composing the poetry as she went along. She kept her eyes fixed on Bartley, and she shook like a field of barley in a breeze when she got into the spirit of singing. A cultured musician would undoubtedly condemn the old people's singing efforts, but the Maker of all music could certainly bless the efforts of the old dear saints to their eternal advantage. I have often been amazed how the Holy Spirit has blessed bad singing to create such excellent saints; and I have marvelled a hundred times over how the evil spirit can curse good singing to create some bad men. The singing at Nant y Gro was not very harmonious, as far as sound is concerned. The harmony was in the old people's spirit. The same tunes were sung a hundred times over, but the old people ensured that they made up for this deficiency by never singing the same tune in the same way. Even though Bartley was eager to have the tune book in front of him, I would say by Mr Cunnah's authority that the hymnbook was often incorrect; but again, Bartley very rarely during his forty years failed to strike the tune correctly. If he was at fault at all perhaps he pitched the tune too high. I heard the old Captain more than once provoking Bartley by saying that many of his pitches were in the chapel's ceiling, and that a few of them had gone through the ceiling to the roof. "That's the reason," said the Captain. "why not a single drop of water ever gets through it."

Like many others, Bartley lost his voice before losing his zeal. That's one of the misfortunes of a precentor compared to an elder – despite advancing in grace, he is not much use when his voice goes. Strangely, everybody knows that a man has lost his voice before the man himself knows it - that is, unless he's wiser than musicians in general. But if Bartley's voice was deteriorating, his zeal for his role increased, and that's the problem in many a church. At long last, Sam Puw and the Captain were appointed to have a brotherly conversation with Bartley regarding the appropriateness of finding him an assistant. Both went to his house one night, and after beating about the bush as gently as possible, Sam Puw said: "You and I have reached a good age now, Bartley; we won't be here forever, you know, and we have to remember that the cause will be here after us. Would it not be better for you to teach someone to be precentor, Bartley; if you were ever called suddenly to the 'heavenly choir,' things would be pretty bleak here in the Nant without anyone to take your place."

"Well, Sam Puw," said Bartley, "my wind, you know, is as good as it ever has been, but I know that the lad from *Llwydiarth* has been eyeing my job for ages. I think you're siding with him. What if I was like Gito Gruffydd who did the job before me? He had the same tune for every measure. I heard him in the same service striking 'The Old Hundredth' at least three times. When the preacher announced the fourth hymn in a long measure all he could do was ask Lot Davies next to him, 'What do I do now?' 'Ah, put another hundred onto it, Gito,'" and that's what he had to do. Maybe if I was more like him I'd get more respect."

"Well, no, Bartley," said the Captain, "we were thinking that you'd like to get one of the lads from chapel to help you. You would still be the head cantor, you know."

"Oh, I see – more of a head than a cantor," said Bartley rather abruptly.

The visit was hardly successful. The two felt rather

disappointed as they returned home. "Do you know what, Sam Puw," said the Captain, "I think that these cantors have been baked on a higher shelf than other people. You might as well try changing the moon than trying to persuade Bartley that his voice is failing. Did you hear the man talking about his wind? Many of us have too much air in us. I don't know what's worse, an elder with no grace or a precentor with no sense. I don't know how Bartley can't see that it's the welfare of the cause that everybody has in mind."

"Well, Captain," said Sam Puw, "we mustn't complain too much about the old fellow, you see, he's sung for forty years on behalf of us both."

"Yes, yes," said the Captain, "that's perfectly true," and both were silent on the subject for many months.

But about that time the Sol-fa became prominent in the area, and because the 'Curwen hotchpotch'[5], as Bartley referred to it, was a foreign language to him, the son of *Llwydiarth Ganol* got the opportunity to step into the limelight. He gathered some of the village children and formed a choir, and won in more than one *eisteddfod*[6], so much that the *Llwydiarth* son's musical genius became the talking point of the whole area. This in turn made the young people even more enthusiastic to have a singing meeting in the chapel. But this greatly angered Bartley, and the situation became very contentious.

---

5   'Curwen' being the last name of the English Congregationalist Minister, Rev John Curwen, who devised the Tonic Sol-fa musical system.

6   An 'Eisteddfod' is a Welsh cultural event where people compete against each other, mainly in the field of literature and music.

Another notable event drove the situation from bad to worse. The son of the *Fron* came home from Liverpool on his holidays and offered the chapel a harmonium out of respect to the cause. Many of the old people where strongly opposed to bringing such a strange instrument into the house of God, and Morus Huws threatened that he would go out if the instrument came in. Between the young people's zeal for the *Llwydiarth*'s son, and the old people's opposition to the gift given by the son of the *Fron*, the authorities found themselves in a dilemma. After lengthy consideration, and much persuasion, it was decided to accept the gift, and the small harmonium was brought in. But the difficulty then was appointing a player. Nobody in the chapel was familiar with musical instruments, but around half a dozen families were eager for their children to be given the honour. Some, admittedly, were more eager for the position to honour their children than for their children to honour the position. One man insisted that his daughter could play with two fingers, and that she was almost able to play with three; whilst another testified that his son could play the Old Hundredth, and two other tunes at least, with both hands. The cause and its success was forgotten by the blind desire of some families to push their children to centre stage. For peace of mind, three unsuitable candidates had to be appointed, and the generosity of the son of the *Fron* proved more of a concern to the cause than a comfort. The poor parents began to think more of their children's good name than the honour of the cause, and a lot of ill-feeling grew between various families. The good has been an occasion for the bad in every age. It was terrible hearing the instrument

going one way and the congregation another. The instrument had often finished before some of the old
people reached the end of the tune. Bartley had more
trouble with the players and their foolish parents than
he had with the *Llwydiarth*'s son.

The authorities saw that things were going from
bad to worse, and an evening was arranged to consider
the situation. The brothers met in the chapel house.
Sam Puw was in the chair. "We must confess," he
said, "that a very wicked spirit is raising its head and
threatening the cause. It's easy to destroy the cause, you
know; but building it up is the difficulty. An oak tree
takes years to grow but can be cut down in a day. When
we were altering our house, any one of us could pull
the walls down. Shon the servant and Janet the maid
could carry the old furniture out. But do you know,
when it came time to rebuild the walls, skilled stone-
masons were needed. You wouldn't imagine how difficult it was to put the old furniture back. The wife took
months getting things in order. And likewise with the
cause. Many can pull it down, but very wise men are
needed to build things up. We need to be very careful
or we will cause a lot of harm, and it's easier to avoid
offense than try to make amends for it later."

"I'm of the exact same opinion as Sam Puw," said
Shon Gruffydd, "you remember the trouble caused
by Maria Morus's thoughtless talk. And even though
she apologized– what's that English word, Captain – I
know that 'polly' is in it anyway; a 'polly' is a bird that
talks, isn't it, without thinking what it's saying. Well,
that's how it was with Maria Morus. She spoke without
thinking, and even though she admitted her mistake,
the cause paid dearly for it, and the wound still isn't

fully healed. Isn't it strange that godly people are so difficult to handle when a small quarrel comes up?"

"Well yes, it is, in one way," said Captain Wiliams, "but remember, no one's sensible all the time. Every one of us is daft enough to be taken to the asylum on some occasions. You need a doctor's certificate to prove that someone's mad, but if we needed a certificate to prove that we were sane it would turn out badly for half of us. Take the man who lives at *Ty Pella,* he's as mad as a hatter when he starts speaking about his children, but you've never seen anyone so wise when handling sheep. Have you noticed how many knowledgeable, intelligent people are foolish and thoughtless? I think that common sense is much better than knowledge and learning. You see, a man doesn't know he's foolish when he's being foolish, any more than a drunk man knows that he's drunk. You need more sense than character for some things, and more character than sense for others. But unfortunately, you need a lot of both for chapel work. If Bartley had the same amount of sense as he has grace, we would do well by him; but very few of us are wise enough to admit that we're foolish."

"Well, well," said Mr Cunnah, with his usual prudence, "we'll have to settle things somehow, there's no good in letting things drag on like this. I was thinking whilst hearing these brothers speak, that the best thing to do is to honour old brother Bartley, he deserves this from us after serving the cause unfailingly for so many years. What do you think of this, that we make him an elder instead of the old shepherd? Everyone acknowledges that he has enough grace, whatever his voice."

Whilst the authorities were in this predicament about how to solve the problem, it seems that other powers were at work untangling the knots. Bartley had a pretty grand-daughter – the daughter of his only son who drowned at sea. She was brought up by her grand-parents, and old Bartley doted on her. The girl, how-ever, had set her heart on the *Llwydiarth*'s son. Mari Bartley had long known about the courtship, but as she knew how her husband felt towards the young man, the relationship was kept secret from him. However, as they were on the verge of getting married, Bartley had to be told. To the grandmother and grand-daugh-ter's delight, the old brother agreed to the marriage, and he turned like a cup in water. Now, the *Llwydiarth*'s son was the man. And if anyone understood music, it was the *Llwydiarth*'s son. He, undoubtedly, was the only one competent to lead the singing at Nant y Gro! The courtship and the marriage proved to be a providential intervention. "I don't know," said the Captain, "wheth-er Providence has anything to do with arranging mar-riages in general, surely not all marriages are evidence of that, but oh my word, it wouldn't be difficult to be-lieve that this marriage is of divine invention. Good luck to them both, I say, what do you say, Sam Puw?"

"Amen to that," said the elder.

And this is how everybody's feelings were sof-tened, apart from those of Morus Huws; he opposed the harmonium until his death. When he was once asked to participate in the prayer service he answered: "Ask her" – pointing at the innocent instrument. The prejudices of good men have been a great hindrance to God's cause, and the reluctance of some godly people has often caused distress. However, the air was cleared at Nant y Gro, the clouds that had been darkening the horizon for months receded, and were replaced with blue skies and the singing of children. The choir of the Nant rose to fame under the guidance of the *Llwydiarth*'s son, and nobody rejoiced more in its success than old Bartley.

CHAPTER VII

THE PREACHERS

The order of lay preachers is well known to all the Nonconformist denominations of Wales, and every denomination is greatly indebted to these men. As you may know, lay preachers are permitted to pursue the affairs of both worlds. For this reason, the combination of a farmer and a preacher, or a merchant and a preacher takes nobody by surprise. Four of these respectable men served Nant y Gro and district; Daniel Elis the farmer, Elias Moses the tailor, Lemuel Morgan the blacksmith and Noah Huws, who kept the corner shop. Their appearance was as strikingly different as their talents.

Daniel Elis was a tall, elegant man about six feet tall with a very dignified appearance. Elias Moses however was short, grey-haired and needle thin. Lemuel Morgan was of average height, broad shouldered and thick necked, and Noah Huws was a 'nice', quiet man with a gentlemanly like appearance. Even though the four looked very different, they all dressed in a very preacherly manner. I don't remember seeing any of them on a Sunday without a soft felt hat and a longer coat than usual. You might see them occasionally heading to their preaching appointments without a white handkerchief, but never without an umbrella, whether rain or shine. These evangelists had to be meticulous about their appearance. In Nant y Gro there were so many people of the same temperament as Barbara

Bartley that I doubt they would receive any means of grace if a man in ordinary clothes stood before them in the pulpit. For them, such a man would be like Elijah without his mantle. Nowadays a preacher can hardly be identified by what he wears but these four men were careful enough to respect the prejudices of their age by accurately adhering to the external appearance expected of them.

For the Saints of Nant y Gro, there was admittedly a charm in the 'mantle'. But remember, it was the man they respected back then and not the clothes he wore. The old people's respect for the cloth stemmed from the honour and sacredness they ascribed to the preacher's vocation. I'm afraid that the present age is in danger of swaying too much in the opposite direction. Nowadays some people think that wearing a white tie is more pretentious than wearing a black one, but from the 'man of the pews' perspective, I would say that venturing into the pulpit is pretentious in itself, no matter how humble the tie is. To 'the man of the seat', the pulpit is special. There is only one pulpit in every chapel, but many pews – and whilst I believe that only a man of exceptional character and ability should stand in the pulpit – I don't believe he should be a 'swank' at the same time. Today, all forms of ritual and ceremony are condemned, and the danger of such an age is to lose devotion and reverence. Perhaps the shadows of bygone days are darkening my mind, but for the life of me I can't see as much piety and awe in today's worship as there used to be. What if the children of Nant y Gro ate sweets in the house of God with the boldness they do today? One glance from Sam Puw would make them choke! And I've never heard anyone talk about preachers as the learned children of today do! My goodness, what if my father heard me say such things? I shudder to think of the anger on his face and the taste of the birch rod, and the scolding to follow!

But to get back to the point, you could guess how each preacher earned his daily bread by the way he conducted himself in the pulpit. You discovered in no time at all that one of them was more familiar with a shovel and pick axe, the other with a needle, the other with a hammer and so forth. Daniel Elis's posture betrayed the fact that his arms were more of a hindrance to him in the pulpit, however useful they were in the fields. It was obvious he didn't have the faintest idea what to do with them. I'm unsure whether the occupation of these four men had anything to do with their status as preachers. I can hardly believe that the old honest saints of the Nant had more respect for Daniel Elis because he was a farmer, or that they had less respect for Elias Moses because he was a tailor, or Lemuel Morgan because he was a blacksmith. But one thing is certain, Daniel Elis was more well respected than Elias Moses, even though the tailor was much more talented and intelligent than the farmer. What accounted for this? I heard Sam Puw, the Captain and Mr. Cunnah discussing it once. The three acknowledged that Elias Moses was far more intelligent. In fact, few dared cross swords with him as he had such skill and dexterity. No one could fault his character, but some of the old saints believed he was too mischievous. As the old Captain said, "We prefer a man with a longer face than usual in the pulpit for the same reason we prefer a black horse at a funeral and a white one at a wedding. For my own part I must say that it's easier to receive means of grace listening to a preacher who has a beard and a bass voice, than to a man with a tenor voice and only a moustache."

"This is how I view it," said Sam Puw. "You see, a man's history is behind him in the pulpit like anywhere else. A man can't ascend into the pulpit like an angel can descend into it – without his history. Everyone knows that Lias Mosus has a better understanding of doctrine than money, and say what you like, people can't listen as well to a man telling them how to deal with the spiritual world when they know full well that he's unable to deal with this world. Lias is a little awkward with the things of this world, anyway. I'm not suggesting that he's a bad tailor, but his sermons are admittedly better than his clothes. They are both made of good stuff, but his sermons are better crafted. And say what you like, a lot of our clothes are tighter fitting than his sermons. And it's easier to forget a sermon than clothes that don't fit properly. And apart from that, the clothes are much more expensive."

"Well," said Mr Cunnah, "I think the old brother is at a disadvantage because of his occupation. Remember that tailoring from house to house, as is the custom in this area, breeds a familiarity that can be a disadvantage. He hears many family secrets, and sees many customs as he goes from house to house, and it's almost inevitable for a man as mischievous as the old fellow to say something that could easily be misinterpreted. If Lias Mosus condemns certain practices, people are less likely to listen as they're bolder with him. An unfamiliar preacher is more able to scold people than somebody who's familiar with our way of life. And another thing, it's natural enough for a man to promise to make clothes, though he knows full well that he'll be unable to keep his word. When people order new clothes they're always in a rush to get them and slow to pay, and the slowest ones to pay are the best at complaining. It's also a great shame that the old tailor uses so many English words when he doesn't know what they mean. Did you hear him say the other Sunday that man is God's mantelpiece? He must have meant 'God's masterpiece', surely?"

"Say what you like," said the Captain. "Lias would be a much better man had he been given a better wife."

"Here we go again," said Mr. Cunnah, the old bachelor. "I don't know what half you married men would do if you had no wives to blame; the sons of Adam are forever holding their wives responsible."

"Well," said the Captain, "as I was saying the other night when I was debating the subject of predestination [7] with Sam Puw, that's why I don't believe the Good Lord is responsible for half these marriages. So many good men, some preachers included, have had such terrible wives; and some bad men have had excellent wives. Do you seriously believe that Heaven would give Lias a wife like Nansi? Even I could make a better match than that. Remember, I'm a great believer in Providence. Providence gifted man with two eyes and sense, but man himself uses those abilities. You think about this now, God gave man eyes, but it's man who sees with them. I'd go so far as to say that Lias Mosus would be a better tailor and preacher had he been given

7   Predestination is the doctrine that all events and situations have been predetermined by God. It was a hotly debated teaching in Welsh Nonconformist Christianity.

a better wife. Look how much of a better a man Daniel Elis is, with less capital in his personality, as that student said last Sunday."

"Well, remember," said Mr. Cunnah, "maybe Daniel Elis was given a better start in life than Lias Mosus."

"No," said Sam Puw, "I have known Daniel since he was a lad. He was brought up in a very simple cottage where money was scarce, but he was always hard-working and thrifty as a boy."

"In my opinion," said the Captain, "he's no better preacher then Lias, maybe even worse. However, he's less eloquent. Do you know, many of us are like an old lady I heard about. She once went to listen to Mr._____, one of the greatest preachers in Wales. 'And this is your great preacher?' she asked when she returned home. 'I didn't think much of him. I understood every word he said from start to finish.' Many of us are the same. Lias is such a good orator, and such a clear thinker, that everybody understands him; but Daniel speaks so slowly, and coughs so often, and his thoughts are so abstract that people are foolish enough to think he's profound."

"But," said Sam Puw, "you must give credit to the poor boy for working himself up the ladder to become one of the greatest freeholders in the area, and without losing his head either. Daniel is an excellent man. I think a man who has succeeded honestly in the things of the world has some authority to speak about the things of the other world. Some people are better preachers than men, and others are better men than preachers."

"Quite right," said the Captain, "and some, like

Dan, make a better farmer than a preacher."

And that's how the three of them were discussing the two preachers. You would do a disservice to Sam Puw for thinking that he and the old saints of Nant y Gro respected Daniel Elis because he was a freeholder. No, they saw the angel in the old blacksmith despite the corns on his hands and the soot on his skin. Everybody acknowledged that the old blacksmith preached very original sermons, and felt that he could make sparks fly in the pulpit as well as at the forge. They also gave deserved value to the talents Elias Moses had. But it must be said, along with Sam Puw, that a careless worker, no matter how talented, was bound to be at a disadvantage when preaching. It's a terrible thing to see a man so spiritual that he forgets to pay his debt in the shop, but never too spiritual to go without food.

As the four of them regularly preached in the same place, they delivered the same sermons over and over. The preachers themselves even acknowledged this. I remember the old blacksmith provoking Noah Huws once. "Where are you going tonight, Noah Huws? "

"To Hermon."

"Oh, so it's the 'Lady from Canaan' they'll hear tonight then. She knows her way there by now."

"That's no better that your 'Three youths,'" said he.

'The Prodigal Son' was Daniel Elis's great sermon, and everyone remembered his description of the younger son returning home 'with one leg on his trousers, one lapel on his coat and no brim on his hat.' One of the old blacksmith's sermons was known as 'The ink bottle' because he described the majesty of

Jesus as follows. "If the trees were writing pens, and the leaves were writing paper, and the big blue sea an ink bottle, you couldn't come within a hundredth, not even a thousandth degree, of describing the beauty of the Lamb."

Preaching the same sermon once lead Noah Huws into a predicament. After arriving at the chapel in good time, he started to wonder whether he had preached the sermon he intended to deliver that night the last time he was there. An observant old man sat near the Great Pew because he was hard of hearing. He was the chapel's 'ready reckoner' and had a phenomenal memory. Noah Huws approached the old man and asked him: "Tell me, what did I have to say the last time I was here?"

"Huh?" said the old brother, raising his hand to his ear. Noah Huws repeated the question slightly louder: "Tell me, what did I have to say the last time I was here?"

"Oh! Well, to be honest with you, you didn't have much to say at all."

Noah Huws was always immaculately dressed. Of the four preachers mentioned, he was the most particular about his appearance. He was the first preacher I ever saw wearing gloves – but there was one event he preferred to keep silent about. He always put great value on punctuality. One Sunday morning, however, he overslept, and between his concern about his sermon and his eagerness to arrive on time he left his house in greater haste than usual. He grabbed what he thought was his top-coat from the bannisters and rushed to his preaching appointment. After travelling a fair distance, he met an old friend. "Where are you going today, Noah Huws," asked the old fellow. "Further than usual, I take it?"

"What made you think that," said Noah Huws. "Well, seeing you with an extra pair of trousers." That's when Noah Huws realised that in his haste he had thrown his trousers over his arm instead of his topcoat. Another rather extraordinary incident happened to Elias Moses. One sunny Sunday afternoon in June the old tailor borrowed a young mare from the man who lived at the *Plas*. The tailor was a rather incompetent horse rider at the best of times, but that morning he was more careless than usual. He let the reins rest on Bess's neck and began reading his sermon. When they passed the millpond, Bess decided that she was thirsty, and was up to her front knees in the water before the preacher realised what had happened. As he tried to grab the reins the old fellow fell headfirst into the pond. Soaked to the skin and covered in mud he was in a terrible state. Bess galloped home in fright and the preacher had to walk home to look for comfort. Instead of preaching that Sunday he had to listen to his wife Nansi's eloquent sermon!

The old blacksmith was admittedly the most original of the four. People often talked about his wittiness, and a lot of innocent fun could be had in his company.

Whilst he was having supper with a minister in the house of a mutual friend, he realised that the lady of the house had forgotten to give him a knife and fork. The minister started to pull his leg: "Well, you'll have to eat with your hands, Lemuel Morgan."

"I'd like to see you try to eat without them, Mr

Puw," he said in a flash.

The old tailor's great virtue as a preacher was his brief sermons, a very uncommon gift back then. Lengthiness was Noah Huws's great expertise. The bad was made worse by the fact that he had fallen into the irksome habit of saying many times over in his sermon, "One small additional word," and "I won't say any more," before proceeding, and always adding many more words to the 'small additional word' mentioned. This caused the old Captain to say once – "Old Noah Huws's sermon is the most perfect idea I have of eternity. He's always on the verge of finishing, and as far from the end when he finally does as when he started."

But in case the reader thinks that I am just as inconclusive as the old preacher, I will finish by telling a story that happened to Elias Moses that caused a lot of excitement at the time. He was troubled by a fear of the dark, and he very rarely ventured out at night without arranging for some friends to accompany him. On the evening in question he had arranged for some friends to come and meet him, but two mischievous scoundrels decided to try and frighten the old brother. On his way home the preacher had to pass through a wooded grove near *Llety Ifan*. The place had a rather oppressive atmosphere, especially on dark nights. The silence was only broken by the croak of a restless raven, or the screech of an owl. It's very unpleasant walking between two high hedges on a country road with nothing but your own footsteps for company. Elias Moses walked briskly that night – he tried humming a few lines to drive away the spirits. He was expecting his friends to arrive any minute, and was reluctant to venture through the grove by himself. He had preached a good sermon that evening, but the service had taken its toll on him, and he was more nervous than usual. Behind a thick bush at the edge of the grove the two scoundrels were lurking, and when the preacher was in close enough proximity they rushed out shouting: "Your money or your life." Like a flash of lightning the preacher spun around and scarpered, and leapt into the lake nearby with an unearthly cry. The boys realised they had overstepped the mark. Luckily the preacher's long expected friends arrived and heard his wails, and with the help of a lantern they found him in good time. The old preacher would certainly have drowned otherwise. The boys ran away, and even though the old brother had his suspicions, nobody knows for certain who they were to this day. The situation greatly disturbed the old preacher and he never ventured out alone at night for the rest of his life.

A friend always travelled with Elias Moses after that, but the preacher's company was enough recompense. "Wmffra my boy," he once asked me, "will you come with me next Sunday to keep me company?"

"All right," I said. We had six miles to walk by ten o'clock, and we arrived in good time. The old fellow was not in good health that Sunday. At the end of his sermon he said that the young man accompanying him would finish the service with a word of prayer. Even though I was used to taking part publicly at home, the request was so out of the blue that I lost all confidence and I had to decline. On leaving the chapel, the preacher was invited to lunch by a tall, thin man, known as "The Old Law." He ignored me. I'm afraid that he had taken offence at my disobedience. "What about the lad?" asked Elias Moses. "Oh yes," said 'The Old Law'.

"Does he profess a faith?"

"Well I know this," said Elias Moses courageously, "he doesn't profess to live without eating." I had lunch in the preacher's shadow that day, but I must say, there was a hint of the law on the old fellow's grace. I never accompanied the preacher on that journey again.

CHAPTER VIII

HUW ELIS THE ANNOUNCER

"Do you think," one of my peers asked me a long time ago, "that there are as many old people today as there were when we were children? You'd be very fortunate today to find a Great Pew full of white-haired old people like there was in the Nant. Do you know, the Great Pew in Nant y Gro was like an Insurance Office. It guaranteed you a long life, a lease on this earth, and a freehold the other side."

"Well," I said, "there's a lot of truth in what you say, my friend. But remember, there are two or three reasons at least for that. To begin with, man through his artistry, to some extent at least, has succeeded in making even old people look younger. Nobody nowadays has to put up with white hair - artistry can change its colour, and provide you with a full set of teeth too. And another thing, people dress so young nowadays. When we were lads, Sam Puw, Shon Gruffydd and old Huw Elis were younger than we are now, but we saw them as old people. We're getting old my friend and the age is getting younger."

When Huw Elis was a man of forty, he looked like a respectable elder. His clothes were old-fashioned, and a razor had never been allowed anywhere near his skin. He walked slowly and clumsily with the steadiness of a man pondering every step. Strangely, you would have thought by his movement and posture that he was a calm, passive man; but if the old brother was slow on his feet he had a quick, fiery temper. He was a carpenter by trade, and as a rule, he made the coffins for everybody in the parish. He had a very high opinion of his trade, and appeared very important and dignified at a funeral. He could be exceptionally serious at such occasions, even though he possessed a good dose of innocent mischievousness. By nature, he was much more like Shon Gruffydd than Sam Puw, even though, of course, he was on excellent terms with Sam Puw. Huw Elis liked to provoke Shon Gruffydd by claiming that carpentry was a far more godly occupation than stonemasonry.

"You never heard of Jesus Christ carving stones, did you Shon Gruffydd," said Huw Elis. "He was a carpenter in Joseph's workshop, wasn't he."

"Well, that's quite true, Huw," the old brother replied. "But I never heard of Jesus Christ making a coffin for anyone either."

"Do you know what, Huw Elis," Elias Moses once said, "I think it's much better you making coffins for the dead than it is for me making clothes for the living."

"Well," said Huw Elis, "that depends a lot on the *man*, Lias."

"Yes, depending on whether he's dead or alive, Huw Elis," the tailor craftily replied.

The old saints had a lot of innocent fun teasing each other like this. Everybody knew that Huw Elis had a very high opinion of his occupation.

Having said that, I'm almost led to believe, that however much Huw Elis valued his trade as a car-

penter, he placed much more value on his role as Announcer in Nant y Gro chapel. Strangely, Huw Elis was
not known as 'Huw Elis the Carpenter,' or 'Huw Elis
the Elder,' but as 'Huw Elis the Announcer.' I can only
ever remember Huw Elis making the announcements.
Nobody ever complained that they couldn't hear him.
He never mumbled, but announced loud enough for
everyone to hear. If a loud voice is an asset in an announcer, then the Archangel mentioned by Paul had
better be on his guard lest he be made redundant in the
Resurrection. Many times whilst announcing at Nant y
Gro, Huw Elis awoke those who were as good as dead.
It would be very difficult I believe to remove Huw Elis
from his post. Of course, I never heard anyone even
suggest such a thing, though I know that more than
one had their eye on the role. Elias Moses made a comment once that earned him Huw Elis's favour for the
rest of his life.

"The announcer's post," said Elias, "is to remain
whilst rivers flow, and the announcer should remain in
post whilst his blood flows."

Huw Elis gave a hearty "Amen" when he heard the
comment.

However, the old brother's memory deteriorat-
ed dramatically during his later years and without the
substantial help received from Shonet his daughter, he
would scarcely have been able to fulfil the role.

It was an unforgivable sin, however, to suggest to
Huw Elis that his memory was failing, and if anybody
other than his daughter interfered with his role as announcer he became very upset. I heard him answering
Sam Puw very abruptly when he happened to correct

one of his announcements, but he would come around in a short while.

Huw Elis was sometimes plagued by depression – an illness always ready to ensnare godly people in every age. As Captain Wiliams said. "Sometimes a lot of us need a bottle of medicine more than we need grace. And at times like that it would be better to pay Doctor Huws a visit instead of tiring the Heavenly King." This was the case with the old brother Huw Elis. You could tell in an instance by the old brother's announcements if his 'liver was out of order.' When he was in good spirits this is how he announced: "Our respectable Minister, Mr. Ifor Jenkins will be with us next Sunday all day." Other times, when he was 'in the dumps', this is what he'd say: "Mr Jenkins will be here next Sunday at ten and six o'clock." – everybody knew then that he was depressed. I heard him announce one brother with an unfamiliar name by pointing at the preacher with his thumb and saying: "We'll have him again at six o'clock tonight."

He knew every preacher on the preaching circuit, and he couldn't refrain sometimes from making suggestive remarks when announcing them. For example: "Such and such will be here next Sunday, *if the weather's good.*" "Morys Prys is *meant* to be here next Sunday," he said another time, "but I heard in town yesterday that he's due to preach in Shiloh on the same Sunday. I don't know what he'll do, but I know that only the omnipresent one can be in two places at once." Many similar examples could be noted.

If a preacher failed to keep his appointment, Huw Elis would be certain to mention the fact when he announced them next time.

Simon Jones the *Voty* was one preacher who often failed to keep his preaching appointments, and Huw Elis, like Jonah in the Old Testament, was very unwilling to announce anything if there was a shadow of a doubt about it.

Some individuals who liked to criticize preachers – and there are many of this family in every age – said that Simon Jones tended to preach where the money was. However, Huw Elis took the matter in hand. Simon Jones was due to preach in the Nant y Gro circuit, and as he was walking along the road in Caerefron one Saturday afternoon, who should come the other way but Huw Elis.

"Wait a minute, Simon Jôs," said the old announcer. "You're meant to be preaching at Nant y Gro a week on Sunday, aren't you?"

"Yes, of course," said the preacher – "Yes, Yes!"

"Well yes, but you'll definitely come, won't you Simon Jôs, or I'll never announce your name again."

"I'm sure to come, brother, if I'm alive."

Sunday came, but not the preacher. Huw Elis felt extremely disappointed. When he announced in the morning service that the evening service would also be a prayer meeting, he said, with great seriousness and solemnity: "You will be very sorry to hear that the old brother Simon Jôs has passed away."

A sadness spread over the entire congregation and the whole area was deeply shocked because Simon Jones, despite all his flaws, was a great favourite of the people.

When Simon Jones heard, towards the middle of the week, that he was dead, he was extremely angry.

He met Huw Elis a short time after that, and said. "Why did you do me such a bad turn, Huw Elis?"

"Well, you're to blame, Simon Jôs," said Huw Elis, "you said so yourself that you would come to preach if you were alive, and I preferred to believe that you were dead, than believe you were lying" – and off he went.

Simon Jones never missed a preaching appointment at Nant y Gro after that.

A prestigious preaching festival was held annually in Caerefron, and the 'announcement' was sent to Huw Elis. The preaching took place outside on the square if the weather was favourable, in Welsh and English, and for the benefit of Mr Hedge and other English speakers Huw Elis made part of his announcement in English: The preaching festival was held over three days. As the weather had been unfavourable once, Huw Elis was asked to announce that the usual English service would not be held on the square, but in the chapel. "There will be no square tomorrow in Caerefron," said the old brother, "it will be in chapel, and one will preach in England and one in Wales."

He reverted to Welsh after the above effort, and in his fluster announced the times incorrectly. "Mr Richards will be preaching at half past six in the evening," said Huw Elis, "and Mr Prydderch at seven." When the old brother made mistakes like this, he couldn't abide being made fun of, but the poor fellow had to suffer a lot of stick, especially from the old Captain.

CHAPTER IX

THE HIGH-FESTIVALS OF NANT Y GRO

The Tea Festival and the Preaching Festival were the two 'red-letter days' at Nant y Gro. The Tea Festival was arranged by the teachers' meeting, whilst the brothers' meeting was responsible for the Preaching Festival.

My greatest ambition when I was still a fairly young lad was to grow up so that I could stay behind at the teachers' meeting. I had heard many times that this was the most important establishment in the entire Kingdom, possibly even more important than the British Parliament. The idea of providing tea for the children was introduced to Nant y Gro by some of the sailors. Some of the old people however felt that such a suggestion was completely contrary to the nature of religion.

"There was no nonsense like this when I was a lad," said the man of the *Fron*, "this tea is nothing but an upper-class luxury."

At least two or three people, who were hardly ever seen at the seiat or the prayer meeting would be exceptionally prominent in the teachers' meeting. Their zeal for the School bordered on being an illness; but whatever fire they had in their souls burnt on this altar alone. They were like burnt cinders on all other occasions.

Many plans, and many more amendments were put

forward in arranging the annual Tea Festival. When
the day dawned, it wasn't the prominent women of
the seiat and prayer meeting who were visible. It's true
that Betsan Puw, Mari Huws, Beti Wiliams and Catrin
Elis were very willing to slice the bread or wash the
dishes; but less faithful women would be in evidence
on that day.

The man of *Ty'nlon* and the man of *Bryniau Bach*
made their great annual appearance at the Thanksgiving Harvest service; but the children's tea was the big
day for the ladies of *Alltwen*, *Llwyndu* and *Coed Tewion*.
The faithful receded into the shadows to give these an-
nuals a chance to blossom in the warm breeze of the
Tea Festival.

Hannah Owen, who lived at *Alltwen* was a very an-
imated lady. There were no limits to her generosity at
the children's Tea Festival, and her bubbling laughter
was contagious. She ensured that the children of Nant
y Gro had thick butter on their bread that day, however
they fared the rest of the year. The ladies of *Llwyndu*
and *Coed Tewion* were equally as energetic as Hannah
Owen. These ladies stored their energy all year and
exploded at the Tea Festival. I must confess as well
that these ladies who made an annual appearance at the
Tea Festival were far more important in the eyes of us
children than the mothers who regularly taught us the
Word of God every week. But then again, everybody
knows that a child's stomach is nearer his heart than
his brains, and older children are very much the same.

There was a very interesting service in the evening.
The choir formed by the *Llwydiarth*'s son performed,
and there were various recitations and competitions.

However, many of the old people viewed such entertainment with a degree of suspicion.

Despite that, the most important day in Nant y Gro's history was the Preaching Festival – the Great Meeting. This was an event in itself, and cast its shadow over every aspect of life in the district. This was the indicator to decide when someone was born or when somebody died.

"Just a minute, how old is Wiliam, now?" the lady of *Ty Newydd* was asked by a friend of hers.

"Well, he was five at the last Preaching Festival. He was born one month before the meeting when Mr. Bonar Evans and that tall young man were preaching. What was his name again? You know who I mean. He was preaching on the verse 'Catch for us the foxes, the little foxes."

"Good gracious, that's another year gone," said the lady of the *Gilfach*, "twelve years ago to this meeting my dear husband was alive. When we were listening to Rolant Dafydd preaching on the verse 'Then shall two be in the field; one shall be taken, and the other left,' neither of us would ever have thought that it would be the last time we would have together."

The Preaching Festival attracted a lot of attention for other reasons too.

"When is the Preaching Festival at the Nant? The weather won't settle until it's happened, you'll see," said the man of *Felin Ucha* to Sam Puw as they walked to the market in Caerefron.

Strangely, the weather was almost always fine for the Preaching Festival, and many believed that the festival actually changed the weather, an important issue in an agricultural area.

The Preaching Festival would be the topic of discussion at Caerefron fair.

"When will you visit us next?" was a common question, and the answer almost inevitably would be: "Well hang on a minute now, the Preaching Festival will be soon, won't it. I might as well wait until then." Nant y Gro's Preaching Festival was the area's almanac.

It even affected the houses. About a month before the meeting you would hear various people asking "when are you going to get lime?"

All the small farmers, and most of the villagers made sure they whitewashed their houses once a year, and the Preaching Festival at Nant y Gro denoted the time. Everybody could be seen at work. There was no need to advertise that the festival was approaching, whitewashing the houses was sufficient notice. And the festival affected not only the houses, but also those who lived in them.

"I have to buy Mari a new dress," one lady said to her husband when he returned home late from work one day, "she's had it now for two meetings."

"When can I have a new hat, mam?" asked another girl, "I haven't had one since that preacher with big teeth was here."

Even though fashion didn't burden the people of Nant y Gro as it does so today, everybody admittedly strived to look their best on the day, and the excuse was regularly heard, "There will be lots of grand people here from the town." I know that my grandmother had

a silk shawl that only ever saw the light of day when
Nant y Gro's preaching festival arrived. I also remember the man of *Ty Newydd*'s speckled waistcoat, which
was as a rule only aired once a year. Then there was the
bonnet worn by the old lady of the *Fron*. She wore the
same one every year, but with annual improvements
added. These items were kept in an oak chest in the
bedchambers, and only the preaching festival was important enough to disturb their silence. As I said before, Nant y Gro's preaching festival cast its shadows
over every aspect of life.

When Huw Elis announced, "Will the brothers
stay behind to choose preachers for the festival," the
words spread like electricity. The brothers' group, as already suggested, had the authority to select preachers.

"I propose," said the man of *Ty Newydd*, "that we
choose one young and one old."

"That will never work," said the man of the *Fron*.
"It would be like putting 'Brown,' the old horse and
'Dick' the young colt in the same harness. They would
never work together." A long time was spent trying to
persuade these two old fellows.

"Well," said Mathew Jones, *Llwyn y Celyn*, "I'll propose Risiart Wmffras as one preacher; do you know, I
liked the sound of his voice when he was here three
years ago, it's been in my ears ever since."

"Nonsense," said the Old Philosopher, "let's have
Arfonydd. We'll get the essence of the Gospel from
him. Isn't there a little calf in the *Geufron* with a nice
voice? But you'll get no sense from a creature like that."

Sam Puw and the Captain had to mediate between

Mathew Jones and the Old Philosopher and the propositions started again.

"I'd like to suggest Huw Morys, *Cae Gors*," said the man of the *Llwydiarth*, "he christened my eldest daughter, and Margiad and I will never forget his prayer."

"With all due respect to the man of the *Llwydiarth*," said Anthony Jones, "it's a preacher we need, not somebody to douse everything in cold water. Many who are good at praying are terrible preachers."

"Yes," said the man of the *Llwydiarth*. "And many gifted with prayer are very lowly people. Don't you, of all people, talk of throwing cold water over things, Anthony."

The chairman begged Anthony Jones and the man of the *Llwydiarth* to keep to the point. "We are discussing which preachers to choose," he said.

After some trouble, and much discussion, two preachers were selected, but some left disappointed.

Finally, the festival arrived. It was held on the first Wednesday night and Thursday in June. To the residents of the Nant, that Wednesday night was like a Saturday night. The sons and servants from the nearby farms flocked down to the village to see the preachers arriving.

"Who went to fetch the preachers this year?" one asked.

"The man of *Llwynon*," replied another. "You should have seen 'Darby' trotting through the village, he was raising his hooves like a year-old foal."

"Yes," said the third. "and you should have seen

how little Dic had polished the harness. It was so shiny you could see your face in it."

"Darby was wearing *Tudraw*'s collar" said another, "and they had the *Fron*'s carriage behind her," said the second.

"Yes," said the third, "and do you know what, Darby and the man of the *Fron* were as smart as each other - "

But before he finished the sentence somebody shouted, "Here they come, lads!" and everybody stared at the road and started listening. I believe the man of *Llwynon* had bought a new whip, and before approaching the turn leading into the village he let Darby taste the end of it so that he would come into the village in style.

Darby, as a rule, could sense even a small hill from far away, and despite the new whip, he slowed his pace before climbing the hill to the chapel. This gave the boys a chance to see the preachers, and they all praised Darby for being so thoughtful!

"Who was the one with the soft hat?" asked one, "didn't he have big hair! How come these preachers have longer hair than ordinary people?"

"Because they have more sense, probably," said another.

"Ah, nonsense," said another, "sense doesn't make hair grow, or else Gito Jones's little donkey would be wiser than his master, who is completely bald."

By seven o clock on Wednesday evening there was no room to move in the old chapel. On Thursday morning, the chapel was full once again. Many travelled there in carriages, some arrived on horseback, and huge numbers came on foot. The people of the Nant were renowned for their hospitality. Every house and cottage was full, and every family, no matter how poor, felt worried and disappointed if the festival passed without them having welcomed anybody.

Nant y Gro chapel was a most spectacular sight at the Great Meeting; and no wonder, because the meeting was everybody's meeting. The servant and the maid could say it was their meeting; and likewise, the simplest smallholding as well as the plentiful farmhouse felt that the Great Meeting of the Nant had something for everyone. 'The men of the sea,' were the only ones who were heard complaining – "It's a terrible shame, I'll miss the meeting this time." Nant y Gro's Preaching Festival drew the village's children home from all directions. Preachers were Nant y Gro's heroes. Portraits of preachers adorned the houses, because the villagers felt that they were the champions of ordinary Welsh people. But like everything else, the Great Meeting passed by, but not without leaving its mark on people's minds. The preachers and their sermons would be the talking point for many weeks to come. At the forge the day after the meeting, the man of *Ty Newydd* and many others could be heard discussing the sermons with the Old Blacksmith.

"What did you think of the preachers this year?" asked one.

"Well, superb," said the man of *Ty Newydd*. "I'm happy to think that I proposed the eldest of the two; I'm sure that Huw Morus is sorry by now that he objected. Wasn't he good!"

"Excellent, definitely" said the others.

"How did you like the youngest of the two?" asked

the Old Blacksmith.

"I liked his appearance very much," said Morgan Dafis, "but the trouble with these young lads is they change God's Word too much. I can't abide them mentioning different translations – there was nothing like this until very recently. What on an earth came over them?"

"I don't have the faintest idea," said the man of *Ty Newydd*, "why preachers, of all people, need to alter the old verses."

"Do you remember, Lemuel, how he read the verse: 'Where the Spirit of the Lord is, there is freedom'?"

"Where the Spirit is Lord there is freedom," said the Old Blacksmith.

"Yes, that was it! Well, where on earth do they get something like that from, Lemuel?" said Morgan Dafis. "I'd rather take my eye from its socket than take a word out of a verse. Haven't they read the verse: 'And if any man shall take away from the words of this prophecy, God shall take away his part out of the book of life'? I'm sure that the college is ruining these lads; give me God's Word as it is."

"Remember, it was the Old Philosopher who insisted on having that young man," said Morgan Davies, "and on my way to the forge this morning I heard that he and these young lads, especially the lad of the *Pandy*, were besotted with him. What will come of the world I don't know. Talking about their 'translations.' What language do they think the Good Lord spoke? Is there any language more original than Welsh, Lemuel?"

"Well, I think Hebrew and Greek are considered

the original languages," said the Old Blacksmith pomp-ously. "I heard Mr. Jenkins the minister explaining once that Aramaic was the language of the ordinary people in the days of Christ."

"They can say what they like about the old verses," said Morgan Dafis. "If I could live the Old Bible as it is, it wouldn't be too bad on me. I know this much, what my mother left was the Bible as it is."

Similar discussions were heard at the workshop of Elias Moses the tailor. "Do you know what," said Elias to a crowd of his friends soon after the meeting, "I always say that I'll never preach after a Great Meeting; seriously, weren't the two excellent."

"Which one did you prefer, Lias Mosus?" asked the son of the *Llwydiarth*. "You're a preacher yourself. You should know."

"Well, to tell you the truth," said Elias, "I don't think it's fair to compare two preachers who were as different as chalk and cheese."

"Yes," said Dick Puw in a flash. "Which was the chalk and which was the cheese? Everybody knows they're different."

"You wait one minute, Dick, you're too sharp," said Elias. "This is what I meant, that there's no point com-paring a horse and a boat? The two are so different, and just as useful as each other in their own way. It wouldn't be right for every preacher to be the same. That would be a disservice to us, and to the Gospel. I liked both, but of course, both appealed to me from a different angle."

"But remember," said the Old Philosopher, "it's

one thing to criticize a preacher, but a different thing altogether to judge a sermon. The older of the two was very doctrinal in his sermon, and it must be said, he was well-versed in his field. If you think about the minister of Moriah, I think he understands dogma better than he understands people. But in my opinion, it's just as important for a successful preacher to understand human nature as it is for him to know his Bible. I must say, that's why I like our Mr. Jenkins. It's easy to see that he understands the philosophy of the mind. Isn't understanding the faculties of the soul just as important to a preacher as understanding syntax and grammar? That boy said excellent things, but he gave the impression of being more of a reader than a thinker. And remember, a man can be knowledgeable without being a thinker."

The Great Meeting had a prominent place in the fellowship that existed among the people of Nant y Gro. One person remembered a particular comment, and another a little story, and it was an opportunity to ponder and reflect.

"Seven years ago to this meeting," said Shon Wiliam from *Llwynderw*, "I found salvation, and these are the best years of my life. As you know, brothers and sisters, I was always a righteous man, like Saul of Tarsus, and thought myself better than half the people in the seiat. But thank God, ("yes, thank God" said Shon Gruffydd) I saw that my selfishness was killing me. Do you remember that story one of the preachers told at the meeting? – I don't remember which preacher exactly, but never mind about that – it was a vivid picture of me before I was saved. He mentioned, didn't he, a king going to a house and asking for something to drink.

A little girl answered the door. 'Could I have a drink please, my girl?' he asked her. She gave no thought to who he was. And the little girl ran to her mother who was doing the laundry in the back. 'There's a stranger there, mam, asking if he can have a drink,' she said. 'There you are, my girl,' replied the mother, quite sternly - you remember the story - 'Here's a cup. Give him some milk.' After the man drank the milk, he filled the cup with money, and the little girl ran to her mother shouting, 'look at what he gave me, mam, a full cup of money!' 'It's a great shame we didn't give him a jug,' said she. Do you know what, I like a little story like that in a sermon; that's what Jesus did, wasn't it? I saw a true picture of myself in the story. That's how I used to be, giving to get something back, turning every stream to my own mill, taking everybody for granted. But thank goodness, things have changed now."

Elin Vaughan rose after him. She had just buried her only son – the breadwinner ever since she lost her husband.

"The morning sermon suited me best," she said: "I thought the sermon 'All things work together for good' was specifically for me. I think there's more life in things in the morning; I don't know how you feel brothers and sisters? Well, you know here in the Nant that I've been under the waves recently, between losing my husband and my only son. I actually thought that I'd angered my Heavenly Father, but thank God," ("yes, thank God," said many on seeing the old sister breaking down) "I saw things in a new light that morning in the meeting and it was a great comfort for me. I saw that God was a Father in the storm as well as in fine weather. Like the preacher said, Job wasn't caught up in tribulations because he was less godly than everybody else - love was testing him, wasn't it? I liked the reference the preacher then made to Jacob - he thought that everything was against him when he lost Joseph and Benjamin, but he came to see that losing Joseph was part of the plans of love. I, my friends, still believe, even though I can't explain it, that the trials I went through are bound to be beneficial for me in the long run."

The festival was the subject of valuable conversation in the seiat for many weeks, and everybody familiar with Welsh village life will admit that Preaching Festivals have been a great blessing in the true sense of the word.

CHAPTER X

TWILIGHT

U p to now we have focused primarily on the people of the pulpit and the great pew. We should now turn our attention to the people of the pews themselves. After all, the pulpit and the great pew exist for the congregation, not the congregation for them. The danger of officialdom, in state and church, is to forget the fact that the people are the final authority. The king exists for the people, and not the people for the king. The same is true of a preacher and an elder, even though some church officials give the impression that everybody exists for their benefit.

"Oh, yes, the people are the *people*," as George Huws said, "and if the soul, or whatever you want to call the thing that unites mankind, started to awake and clench its fist, institutional oppression would soon stop."

This 'thing' has admittedly awoken a great deal since the days of George Huws, to the terror of prejudices and superstition.

Fifty years ago, social differences were much more apparent in Nant y Gro than they are today. You only had to look at how the congregants dressed, and indeed, at the pews they sat in, and you could instantly tell who was the master and who was the servant, who were the rich and who were the poor. Wealth and poverty forced their way into the sanctuary; the poor sat

on bare, simple benches, whilst the proud and wealthy
demanded pews with comfortable cushions. This old
injustice is aired in the old couplet:

"Letting pews to the rich,
Leaving the poor on the floor."

Nant y Gro had it's 'petty gentry' – that is, wealthy
farmers or cosy old sailors who had retired from the
sea and turned to farming more for pleasure than prof-
it. It's true that most were 'honorary members' more
than anything else; people who were suffered, mainly, for their money. They were of very little service,
apart from the fact that one might take the chair at a
missionary meeting, and another might preside over a
lecture or a concert. They were fairly generous at such
occasions, and at times like this were considered not
completely worthless to the cause after all.

Of course, the 'petty gentry' of the chapel are
nothing but a second edition of the 'petty gentry' of
the church, and it could be said that the second edition
is also a cheaper edition. There were glorious exceptions remember. Sam Puw, Mr Cunnah and the Captain
could boast of the things of this world, but these men
had greater things to delight in. Many of the chapel's
petty gentry were distressed that they had so many poor
relations, and even though they didn't acknowledge the
relationship, they couldn't deny it either. Their poor
relations reminded them of their beginnings. Their relationship with the chapel was similar. They thought
of the chapel as 'one of father's poor relations' that
had to be acknowledged. There were of course wonderful exceptions. Even though this class of people
was not an integral part of chapel life at Nant y Gro,

they nonetheless created an atmosphere of some sort that unconsciously influenced chapel life. They would flock to the chapel on the first Sunday of the month to hear the minister, and their presence created an air of heartfelt reserve. On the other hand, their absence on ordinary Sundays would speak volumes and the empty pews were in stark contrast to the full benches. That is, the bare benches were full every Sunday, no matter who was preaching, but the wealthy had their select preachers. It's a good thing that chapels are now designed in a way that has done a lot to alleviate this injustice. All pews are now identical, and the hard old backless benches have been banished. But I still don't believe that the best pews should be reserved for those who can pay the highest price for them, especially if they're unfaithful. Give a grave if you like to the highest bidder, but give a seat in God's House to those who make the best use of it.

The greatest surprise about the poor of Nant y Gro is that they appeared so happy in their hardship, and so content in their poverty. They respected the wealthy with a measure of fear that bordered on servility. Many of the petty gentry admittedly appeared generous, especially in times of hardship. They paid low wages to their servants, but could be very charitable. Astonishingly, the religious poor of Nant y Gro could live so contentedly on charity, when they could legally demand their comforts as rights.

Of course, farm servants back then had very little time to read and think for themselves. As a rule, they received their ideas, like their wages, unbegrudgingly from their masters, and if the master could shape the ideas of the ordinary people, it was a very easy task to set the wage. The most wonderful feelings existed between master and servant. It was enough for servants and maids back then to be in their masters' favour and approval. They never realised that they had a right to live. They thought of living as a favour more than anything else.

Not everyone wishes to live in sunlight, however. Some find its brightness distressing, and prefer the grey light of the moon. "Why don't you come to chapel as a family on these fine evenings?" Shon Gruffydd once asked a poor widow he visited. "Well, to tell you the truth, Shon Gruffydd," she replied, "it's too light now. On dark evenings I can cover the children and myself in something, but these light evenings reveal everything." The rush-candle used to hide the poverty of many a cottage, and in its weak light the bad looked rather good. The cottagers of Nant y Gro lived in their own light in more than one sense. The women gathered rushes in their season not only to roof their houses but also to light their homes. They sheltered beneath the rushes, and contemplated in its light. The rush-candle played its part in driving away the darkness, but its orbit was extremely small.

Another light came to the area uninvited, and received very little welcome. George and Mari Huws reared a little boy. He came to them when he was still a fairly young child; no one knew from where, and nobody knew who his parents were. Everybody believed he was of good stock, and it must be said he had a rather aristocratic appearance. It was suggested that his mother was a local girl who went to England to work as a domestic servant. Willie Moreton's childhood was shrouded by mystery that challenged the area's norms. One thing was obvious – money came from somewhere for his upkeep. For four years he walked to the school in Caerefron, and he spent two years at a school in England. The intention was for him to be a doctor, but he chose instead to live on the monthly amounts that came regularly from somewhere for his maintenance. However, he matured into a thoughtful boy. Books were his companions, and some taunted him that he always had his nose in a book and was too lazy to work. He became a very independent minded young man, and indulged in ideas that were strange, if not shocking to most of the area. He found in George Huws an avid supporter. Shortly after returning to the area from school, he was involved in a confrontation with the parish Vicar. It appears that the Vicar was a Justice of the Peace and that the case of some tramp had been brought before him. He was accused of sleeping rough and sentenced to fourteen days in prison. When Willie Moreton met the Vicar he criticized him harshly.

"What sense is there," said Willie, "in imprisoning a man for sleeping rough? Have you not heard of One 'who had no place to lay his head'? It's a good thing that magistrates back then were not as cruel as you, or the Good Lord Himself would probably have been given fourteen days."

Willie Moreton's ideas caused a lot of trouble for the leaders of Nant y Gro Chapel. The man of the *Plas* took part in a prayer meeting one night, and after he finished, his servant started praying. The man of the *Plas* placed great emphasis in his prayer on the fact that we are all children of the same Father, that we all eat at the same table and are all brothers. He was a gracious, kind hearted old fellow and, according to the standards of the age and the area, was a devout Christian. When Willie Moreton heard him saying in his prayer that we all eat at the same table, it crossed his mind that there were two tables at the *Plas* – the family table by the fire, and the men's table by the window. He knew that the servants' bread was much blacker than the bread the family ate. He also remembered that Lewis Morus, the servant, was responsible for the small table at his own home, and he also knew that his wife and children were often hungry. Willie walked home that night with the good-natured man of the *Plas*, and asked him: "Are you not bothered sometimes by your wealth and Lewis Morus' poverty? How would you like to see your eldest son with plenty, and your youngest in poverty?"

"Oh, I'll look after both equally, Willie Moreton."

"Well, it's very admirable that you have impartial feelings as a father," said Willie Moreton, "but what would you think of somebody who would dare stop you acting on those feelings?"

"You tell me, who has the right to step between my children and I?"

"But what if the eldest boy was more fortunate in the things of the world than his younger brother? Would you not expect the eldest to be compassionate towards the younger one?"

"Yes, I guess."

"Quite so," said Willie Moreton, "God is a Father to you and Lewis Morus, and as you're both brothers, does not the poverty of Lewis Morus and his family bother you sometimes?"

The man of the *Plas* felt the blow, and when he was asked to take part in a prayer meeting shortly after, he shook his head, and Sam Puw and Mr Cunnah were informed why. This is how Willie Moreton was somewhat of a hindrance to the leaders.

After much suffering, Sam Puw and Mr. Cunnah visited him, and both tried to persuade him not to stir up trouble. "We're used to things as they are, you see, Willie Moreton," said Sam Puw, "and we're all fairly comfortable, and satisfied with our lives."

"Yes, that's the problem," said Willie, "I was talking the other day to Beti Wiliam, persuading her to try and rouse more ambition in her children, and that's what she said: 'This is how things are meant to be, my boy, this is how they were before you were born, and this is how they'll be after you're buried.' I wonder, Sam Puw, whether you, as religious leaders, are to blame that these people are so satisfied with their poverty? I'm afraid that, unintentionally, you give them the impression that poverty is a virtue. You heard how Huw Lewis who lives at the *Ddôl* was rejoicing in his poverty at the last seiat. He explicitly said that he was completely satisfied with his poverty and his cottage, because, 'a house not made with hands, eternal in the heavens,' has been promised him on the other side. What wonder he spoke like that after hearing Daniel Elis preaching the previous Sunday on the verse: 'I have learned, in whatsoever state I am, to be content.' It's easy enough for him to encourage men like Owain Wiliams, Huw Llwyd and Huw Lewis to be content in their poverty, when he's left the cottage and become a wealthy freeholder."

"Well, yes, but you remember, Willie," said Sam Puw, "that the road from the cottage to the palace is open to everyone who'll work for it."

"Quite right, Sam Puw, that's what I want, but unfortunately these people think that they're poor according to God's will, and then they lie down beneath their burdens, and whilst they believe that God chooses them to be poor, they're bound to feel it's a virtue to effortlessly submit under their burdens."

"Someone has to be servant, and someone has to be master," said Sam Puw; "if everybody wanted to be master what would come of the world?"

"Yes of course, Sam Puw," said Willie humbly, "I don't want men not to be servants. I want the servant to be acknowledged as a man and refuse to be poor. The man must be awoken in the servant; religion doesn't deprive man of his right to think, and neither heaven nor earth can save a thoughtless man from sin or poverty either."

Mr Cunnah was not as patient as Sam Puw. He turned to Willie Moreton and said that he was not the man to talk about such impractical things. "Not everybody's as lucky as you, Willie Moreton; you don't have to earn your daily bread. Nobody should eat bread they haven't earned. Somebody must pay more for it as you get it for free. Do you know what the Bible says about this? 'That if any would not work, neither should he eat.' But the trouble is that the idle worker is often the greediest at the table."

The remark cut Willie, but he stood his ground. "My message gives me a right to live, Mr Cunnah," he said, "and a thinker should definitely receive his bread.

I try to live to think for the poor in this area. Yes, I'm called an infidel, but I can assure you that it's zeal for God's honour that leads me to persuade these people that He is not responsible for their poverty. Have you ever heard the concept, Mr Cunnah – 'every man for himself and God for us all, as the elephant said when he danced among the chickens'? It's easy for the elephant to say that, but what about the chickens?"

Even though Willie Moreton lived for the poor and was kinder than anyone, all his efforts were misunderstood. "That lad's losing his head after being in England," said Beti Wiliam, and that's what most people thought about him, so much that they resented seeing him come to chapel because so many of the area's wealthy men were hostile to him and his ideas. But despite all opposition, he stuck to his message. Only one daily newspaper came to the area, and that was for Willie. He was the district's newsagent, and many came to his lodgings to learn what was going on in the world. Even though the wealthy were hostile to Willie, and the poor suspicious of him, everybody had something to say to him, and many desired his company, though not publicly for fear of the powerful. The pitiful condition of some of the district's godly old people was bound to appeal to a thoughtful man, and Willie Moreton, unfortunately for him, was fifty years ahead of his time. He visited people's houses, and even though many of them appeared fairly content, he was worried on discovering their abject poverty. "In the name of humanity," said Willie, "something's wrong somewhere; the hard-working and industrious should not be poor, according to the Scriptures." It was only love for the poor that made him feel for them. He also succeeded in rousing some and angering others. Many houses in the area, despite being clean, were in a deplorable condition. It's true that nature did them a favour by allowing flowers to grow to hide the walls, but flowers can't hide poverty or drive it away either.

Many cottages in the neighbourhood were made of mud, with mud walls, mud floors and a roof of straw or rushes; however, they contained content families, and as a rule, a great number of children. It could be said of them:

"Oh, fair cottages of Wales,
Smiling by the stream,
The gardens full of flowers,
And the houses full of children."

And the following lines are equally as true:

"O grey cottages of Wales,
Sheltering beneath the trees,
Though their walls are not of marble,
And their roofs are straw or rushes,
Inside are many angels
Who exuberantly gaze,
With awe and jubilation
At the inheritors of Heaven."

A lilac tree and red roses grew in front of every house, and very few homes neglected family prayers. What wonder that angels doted on seeing the large family of the small cottage kneeling on the mud floor in front of Almighty God. You would have thought that it would be easier to thank God on a wooden floor in a cosy farmhouse than on the mud floor of a lowly cottage; but judging by the prayers and experiences of the saints of Nant y Gro, the thanksgiving of the cottage was much sweeter.

It was wonderful to notice the trust they had in one another. You would almost think that poverty is better than wealth for bonding people together. Huw Morus once lost his cow – the small family's main source of livelihood. He was given an opportunity to buy a new one for a reasonable price from the man of the *Plas*. As he didn't have enough money to pay, he shouted at Shon Llwyd, his neighbour who lived across the river, if he could borrow five pounds. Shon Llwyd tied the cord around the neck of his ancient money-pouch and without a second thought threw it across the river without a note of hand or anything else as evidence of the loan. On notable occasions, it wasn't uncommon to see a neighbour wearing his friend's clothes. They regularly borrowed each other's clothes for weddings or funerals. They lived in different cottages, but the love between them was so great they were like one family.

It was interesting to note the familiarity with which they addressed their Heavenly Father in the sanctuary. What would this fashionable age think of old Huw Morus' payer at the Harvest Thanksgiving service:- "Thank you, Lord, for the good corn You have given us, and for the glorious hay, and the wonderful fruit; they are worthy of You, but honestly, Great Lord, Your potatoes aren't very good this year." I well remember the prayer old Shon Pyrs said one Sunday morning. The preacher with a wooden leg was meant to preach that Sunday, but he failed to keep his appointment. Shon Pyrs was asked to pray. "We come before you again, Great Lord," said the old brother, "with a small thank you. We have nobody else today, your servant has let us down. We don't know what happened to him, but you do. Maybe someone asked him to preach at a larger place, and offered him more for his trouble. If so, Lord, forgive his greed. But maybe he's had an accident, and broken his leg, poor soul. If so, Great Lord, have mercy on him, you know he only had one leg before, and forgive us for doubting him."

As a rule, Beti Wiliam and Mari Huws were exceptionally gifted at the seiat, but one evening Beti happened to be feeling rather under the weather. The reason for that (even though nobody knew at the time) was as follows: She had sent Owain Wiliam, her husband, to town with a basket of butter. Beti's last words to him as he set out were: "Remember to bring it back unless you get eighteen pence for it." Rather than take the basket to the shop, the old fellow decided to hide it in some shrubbery above the village, and went first to ask about price. After sounding out the market he came back to collect the basket, but to his great distress found that a greedy old sow had discovered it and eaten the butter – this is what anguished the old lady. But she went to the seiat despite that. "Well, dear Beti," said Sam Puw, "how are you feeling tonight?" As the shadow of the misfortune had not yet lifted from her spirit, she was extremely hard on herself. She was worried that she had no religion at all. Sam Puw knew how to handle her. "Well, dear Beti," said the old elder, "if I were in your place I would give up my religion all together. A religion like that is more pain than pleasure."

"What did you say, Sam Puw?" said the old lady excitedly. "I would never exchange my tiny bit of religion for anything I've ever seen. Good gracious, Sam Puw, what would become of me without it?" The old lady started to rejoice and forgot about her loss, and Sam Puw achieved his goal.

But despite the old fellow's skill in leading the sei-at, even he was cornered once. There belonged to the chapel an elderly lady named Sara Morus. She was a spinster, and not through choice, either. She worked as a domestic servant for the old respectable widow-er who lived at the *Fronchwith*. Sara was of impeccable character, and was also considered to be exceptionally good at her work. Yet again, there was something in-nocent about her. People who live off things like this believed that the man of the *Fronchwith* should have a wife to look after his motherless children, and that he could find nobody better than Sara. She was of the same opinion, even though she pretended to take great offence if anyone dared suggest it.

Gossip like this was not part of Sam Puw's world, and his Puritanical mind was too spiritual to even con-sider such stories. This is how he fell into misfortune one evening at the seiat. The saints were not as talka-tive as usual, and some fairly prominent members also happened to be at home ill. A seiat such as this one, a 'tooth extraction seiat' as they are called, is extremely tedious for an elder. That is, trying to get people to talk almost reluctantly, or the elder having to spend the whole evening speaking himself. This seiat happened to be one of those. He had to ask question after ques-tion. He came to Sara Morus: "Well, sister, it's good to see you in the house again. You love the house, don't you?"

"Oh, yes," said she.

"Yes, very good; loving the house is good, but what about the things of the house? Do you love these?"

"Yes, sir," said Sara nervously.

"Well, it's good to love the house, and loving the Bible and the ordinances of the house is vital. But you love the man of the house, don't you, Sara?"

"Good gracious, Sam Puw, it's not fair to bring things like that up in the seiat," said Sara excitedly. Sam Puw and poor Sara were obviously not talking about the same man.

CHAPTER XI

GEORGE HUWS' FAMILY

Mari Huws was known as the wife of George Huws the Weaver. The custom in the area as a rule was to call people by their first name, coupled with the name of their house or occupation; such as Wiliam *Ty Hen*, or Dafydd the Shepherd, or Margiad the Mill and so forth. For some reason, however, George and Mari Huws were addressed by their full names. Strangely, their children were also always called by their first and second names. I'm unsure whether the preacher's comments when he baptised their first child had anything to do with this but I remember him saying: "I baptize you, Robert Arthur," before adding, "yes, remember that Robert Arthur is the child's proper name, and that he's as much Arthur as he is Robert, and as much Robert as he is Arthur." The family accepted the advice, and the area followed suit. Whilst the other children were usually only called by their first names, and sometimes by only a part of their first name, such as 'Dicw *Ty Gwyn*', and 'Wil *y Foel*' the children of George Huws from the *Pandy*[8] were known as 'Robert Arthur,' and 'Mary Ellen.'

There was something rather devotional about Mari Huws, and she was exceptionally sensitive to other peoples' feelings. She greeted everybody by their prop-

---

8   *'Pandy' is the Welsh word for 'fulling-mill' – where wool was prepared for weaving.*

er names, and thinking about it, I don't think I ever heard her refer to the Saviour without using his full name; and I'm doubtful that I heard anyone utter the name "Jesus Christ" as beautifully as Mari Huws did. She said it with such charm it made your heart glow.

Whereas George Huws was a skilful weaver, Mari Huws was considered an expert with the small spinning wheel. It was as if she had two right hands, and was very nimble fingered. You never saw anyone so diligent. I don't ever remember seeing her, apart from on a Sunday, without her knitting needles and a ball of yarn tied to her belt. She made clothes for her children, and stitched every item worn by her family, apart from George Huws' best clothes.

Mari Huws dressed according to the old custom of the area in a petticoat and bedgown [9]. She wore an old Welsh hat that resembled a sugar-loaf with a white cap beneath it and the two prettiest white frills my eyes have ever seen. This attire suited her, much better than it suited Beti Wiliam. Beti was a short, fat lady with a round face, and was rather late at the market to choose a nose. But as for Mari Huws, she was taller than average, with a strong face and a prominent roman nose. The two white frills each side of her face gave her nose a sense of proportion - that is, it would look bigger without the frills.

Mari Huws was from an old noble family, and ordinary circumstances had failed to make the slightest impact on her nobility. Her only flaw was that she boasted about her lineage. I heard her say many a time that

9   *A type of jacket for women which has short sides at the front and a long tail at the back.*

she was a descendant of one of the old Welsh Barons, though nobody doubted the validity of the claim. Unbeknown to her, her posture and demeanour suggested nobility, and everybody believed that the baron gained more honour as a result of her character, than he contributed to her through his wealth. She was one of the most rational ladies in the area, but her greatest asset was her unquestionable piety. Her presence created a warm atmosphere at home and in chapel. As the old Captain said in his nautical language: "Some people are like icebergs and change the weather, sending a chill over everyone, but Mari is like the Gulf Stream bringing warmth with her everywhere she goes." There was only one person who doubted her godliness, and that was Mari herself.

George Huws was a quiet man of strong convictions and had the reputation of being an avid reader. Even though Mari Huws could speak eloquently at the seiat, George Huws rarely spoke apart from at family prayers, alternately with his wife. But George Huws was master of his household. I don't think I ever saw a father who had better control over his children. The children had chores at specific times. Every Saturday Robert Arthur could be seen chopping firewood and sweeping the yard and it would be easier to stop a shower of rain than to lure him from his duties. Many of the mothers often scolded their children by using Robert Arthur as an example but to have a boy like Robert Arthur you needed a mother like Mari Huws. She had disciplined her children well. The whole family were always in chapel together.

One Monday evening a missions meeting was held at Nant y Gro. A famous missionary took part who had spent over twenty years in India. George Huws was sitting near the door of the pew with his head in his hand. Next to him sat Mary Ellen, then Mari Huws, then Robert Arthur at the far end of the pew next to his mother – that was how they always sat. The missionary appealed fervently not only for people to give money towards the work, but for parents to offer their children. "I wonder, is there any boy here tonight who would dedicate himself to the work? How long must we wait for a missionary from the ancient church of Nant y Gro?" The earnest pleas touched Robert Arthur's heart, and he decided in the pew that night that he wanted to be a missionary.

This is one occasion where Mari Huws doubted her piety! "Mam," said Robert Arthur, "I want to go to India to preach Jesus Christ as Saviour to the Indians." India was very far for Mari Huws, much further than heaven. She knew that only a river stood between her and heaven, but she had heard that oceans and continents separated her from India. Her mind started to rebel, and instinct started wrestling with grace. She was very fond of Jesus Christ, but on the other hand she loved her only son. When the children went to bed that night, Mari Huws and her husband had an intense discussion: "What shall we do?" asked Mari Huws, "Robert Arthur wants to be a missionary." George Huws wasn't in very good health at the time, so Robert Arthur's help at home in the *Pandy* was invaluable. "Well, well," said George Huws, "I don't know what I'll do without him."

"Well, remember, George Huws, the Lord is asking for him."

"Oh yes, I know that, but why does Heaven ask

more from us than from other people? We only have one son, there are five in ..." But before he could finish his sentence Mari Huws interrupted: "Yes, of course, there was only one Son in Heaven too, George Huws, when your case and mine was in the balance."

Even though the thought of saying farewell to Robert Arthur caused Mari Huws great heartache, she involuntarily found herself arguing in favour of the calling to India.

On their knees in the dead of night they received God's help to submit to the calling, and that night Robert Arthur was presented to God and the mission work by solemn parents.

In due time, Robert Arthur took the preparatory course, and the farewell meeting will be long remembered. It is difficult to describe the day of his departure. It's enough to say that Mari Huws had packed his box with her own hands, and that her tears and prayers had consecrated everything put into it. Robert Arthur received a handsome Bible from the people of the chapel, and when he saw his mother placing it on top of the pile in the chest, he asked her suddenly, "Could I have your Bible, Mam, instead of this one?" Robert Arthur knew that there was more in his mother's Bible than in the new one. Her tears and fingerprints had imprinted his mother's history into it. "A Bible with my mother in it will help me in India," said Robert Arthur to himself. He could say about his Mother's Bible along with the poet:

"There are teardrops on its pages,
Never will they fade away,
And she's folded many corners

To mark verses, here and there.
As she read its revelations
Tears would fall a hundredfold,
As she wept in exultation
Feasting on those words of old."

Sam Puw and Captain Wiliams went with George Huws to accompany Robert Arthur to London. George Huws conducted himself courageously whilst Robert Arthur was in sight, but when he left his son on the ship he broke down completely and wept bitterly. Strangely, Mari Huws managed to keep herself composed. She had fought her greatest battle that night when she triumphed in prayer.

Mari Huws and the Captain had always been great friends, but when Robert Arthur left for India the Captain's company became more valuable than ever, because he had been in India many times. Mari Huws bombarded him with thousands of questions about the country and the people, and "Bombay", "Calcutta" and many other long and unfamiliar names became completely familiar to her. Through her son's letters, she familiarised herself with India, so much that I believe she had an accurate map of the country written on her heart.

Robert Arthur's departure was a means to broaden the mental horizons of the congregation of Nant y Gro. This was apparent immediately in the prayers. The 'black man' and 'pagan' occupied a great portion of the prayers, and the missionaries were never forgotten. Robert Arthur's departure gave a new tone to church life, and his departure in fact provided an entry. When Robert Arthur left the chapel, India came in.

The young missionary worked hard in his new field, and gained a respectable position amongst the giants of the faith. He was given the privilege, among other things, of translating parts of God's Word into the language of the natives. He regularly wrote to Sam Puw, and the old elder read out his letters to the great delight of the congregation. Robert Arthur had more influence in Nant y Gro when he was in India than he ever had at home. His letters inspired more missionary zeal in the chapel than anyone could have imagined.

After labouring in India for over a decade, Mari Huws received a letter from him stating that he hoped to make a visit home. His family and the congregation of Nant y Gro were overjoyed at the thought of welcoming home their hero. Word came that he had started, but intended to visit South Africa on his way home. George Huws and the family were in high spirits thinking of welcoming their only son. They busied themselves in preparation. He intended to arrive early in July; the house had to be whitewashed, and both mother and daughter were bustling about. Robert Arthur's arrival decided everything. "When can we dig the potatoes up, and collect the green beans, Mam?" asked Mary Ellen. Oh! They would have to wait until Robert Arthur returned. Homecooked ham hung from the ceiling, but it could no way be sliced until Robert Arthur was home. He was to receive the first fruits of everything.

The *Pandy*'s kitchen was always clean, but Mari Huws and Mary Ellen worked morning and evening giving everything an extra scrub. And remember, there were thousands of small trinkets to clean.

Daniel Ddu o Fôn [10] describes the kitchen of his childhood home in his wonderful poem "My Parents' Home," and the image is a fairly accurate one of the kitchen at the *Pandy*.

> "The cleanest kitchen – have I ever seen
> A place I so adored – in the whole world?
> My love towards it steadily increased
> As I heard the wind sweep through the woods;
> Its floor was covered with the finest sand,
> And all the furniture was in order,
> The tables white, the chairs clean,
> And everything in its appropriate place;
> The handsome clock, crowned with a nest of eggs,
> The old dresser and the large metal bowls.
> The great cauldron, and the copper pans,
> The gleaming bowls, and the clean bronze plates,
> And on the mantelpiece above the fire
> Shone the muzzle, spurs and stirrups.
> Hanging from the roof, all bent and knotted,
> Was my grandfather's walking stick,
> And my mother's medicinal leaves,
> To cure ailments of all kind."

The kitchen implements and furniture were always clean, but the brass candlesticks on the mantelpiece shone brighter than usual and the copper kettle was so bright you could see your reflection in it. The plates on the oak dresser, and the clasps on the Bible on the round table were as clean as 'elbow grease' could get them. Tango, the poor dog, wasn't allowed anywhere near the house, and Thomas John, the cat, had to sneak carefully to his usual spot on top of the range. Whilst George Huws watched the weaver's shuttle working,

---

10   *A Welsh poet – 'Black Daniel of Anglesey'*

the old fellow started singing Herber's old hymn to the clicks of the weaver's beam:

"From Greenland's icy mountains,
From India's coral strand;
Where Africa's sunny fountains
Roll down their golden sand"

Was not his son returning home; and wasn't he that very moment weaving fine cloth from the wool of the Welsh mountain sheep to make him a suit!

They were wondering in the *Pandy* what Robert Arthur would look like. They knew his health had failed him, but Mari Huws had been rearing chickens for many weeks to feed her beloved son.

Before leaving for India, Robert Arthur had secretly promised Sam Puw's daughter Gwen that he would be faithful to her, but they were the only ones who knew of this promise. He intended to seal the covenant with a ring on his return.

The villagers of Nant y Gro went to bed early. It was the area's custom to follow the sun. That night, shortly after nine o'clock, George Huws and his wife were talking later than usual; and Robert Arthur's return was the topic of conversation.

"I'm worried that he would have lost a lot of weight in that hot country," said Mari Huws. "I had a horrible dream about him the other night. I saw him in great danger, and I clearly heard him shout 'Mam.'"

"Don't worry, my girl." said George Huws, "With dreams, it's always the opposite that's true. When he's home we'll fatten him up in no time. There's nothing like the fresh air of home."

"Yes, that's true," said Mari Huws, "If only I had my dear son to look after again. He'll get the best I can give him, but it's taking so long."

"Isn't all waiting long?" said George Huws.

Whilst they were both talking in the twilight, with the rush-candle nearly extinguished, Tango the dog stared barking and there was a knock at the door, and the noise of somebody's hand on the latch, and then Sam Puw's voice was heard:

"You're not in bed, are you?"

"Good gracious, what brought you here at this time of night?" said George Huws. "Oh hello! Mr Jenkins, you're here too, where on earth did you come from?" Mr Jenkins the minister had travelled there from Caerefron. "Dear me, my good men." said Mari Huws, - "Fetch them a chair, George Huws – get out of the way, Tango, and go to your kennel – take this armchair, Mr Jenkins, what brought you here at this time of night? Not bad news I hope?"

Mari Huws' instincts awoke and she sensed that something was wrong. "Is Robert Arthur all right, Sam Puw?" she asked, stretching for the candle. Mari Huws noticed that Sam Puw's face was whiter than usual, and she felt something worrisome in the minister's cautious voice. "Tell me at once," said Mari Huws, "Is my dear boy all right?"

"Well, my dear friends," said the minister slowly, "things are not as we wished. Robert Arthur has been taken ill."

"But is he alive?" asked Mari Huws mournfully.

"Well, friends, it's difficult to say this, but Jesus Christ has called him home."

George Huws and his wife were dumbfounded. There was not a tear or a language to express their grief, and that's the second time Mari Huws doubted her piety! She felt for a moment that Heaven was further than India, because there was no hope that Robert Arthur would ever return. Mari Huws looked deep into her husband's eyes as if she was paralysed; she wept in her heart as Hannah did in the Old Testament. "Only her lips moved, but her voice was not heard." The four were speechless! Mari Huws was the first to break the deafening silence: "What do you say to something like this, George Huws?" she said.

"Well," said George Huws slowly, "My only concern is that I'm not twenty years younger so that I could go to India to finish the work started by my dear son. The only thing is, I don't have another boy to give."

The four knelt down, and a light brighter than the rush-candle shone on them; Mari Huws let her feelings flow in holy tears, and George Huws began blessing God that he was able to raise a boy to do such glorious work.

The following morning, the bad news was broken to the village, and the villagers flocked to the *Pandy* to offer their condolences. The family's hopes were shattered, and Gwen, Sam Puw's daughter, had to bury her desires. Burying a body in the earth is nothing compared to burying hope in a broken heart. Robert Arthur's body was laid to rest under a lonely yew tree in the African sands. His body was unable to be brought home, but his soul made the journey.

Behind the pulpit at Nant y Gro chapel stands a beautiful plaque, and on it these words:

IN MEMORY OF THE LATE

REV. ROBERT ARTHUR Huws

A MISSIONARY IN INDIA, &C . . &C

A letter arrived explaining his illness in more detail. His last words were, "Remember me to mam and Gwen."

Shortly after this sad event the water wheels of the *Pandy* stopped turning, and George Huws was taken ill. He also found himself in straitened circumstances, and concerns about his livelihood added to the tremendous pain he suffered from arthritis. Many times he asked in his illness. "What will become of us? The wheel of the *Pandy* hasn't turned in months."

"Don't worry, father," said Mary Ellen. "I'll find work as a maid, and look after you and mam." The girl found a place in England. She turned out to be as much of a heroine in her circle as her renowned brother. She saved her wages to provide for her parents, but her friends taunted her that she was too miserly to live. Her self-sacrifice was misinterpreted, but she kept her parents' poverty a secret despite all misunderstandings.

"It's shameful that you wear that same old hat summer and winter, Mary Ellen," said one of her peers as she left chapel one Sunday evening. "Doesn't Mary Ellen look shabby," said another two a short while later. She suffered everything in silence. But there was nobody as content as her in town. Whilst her friends sought out selfish pleasures, she enjoyed saving her money for her mother and father. Every month sent a Post Office Order home, and when she received a letter with teardrops on the pages – the imprint of her parents' thanksgiving – she was strengthened to persevere in the face of every taunt and misunderstanding. "If they don't understand me here, they understand me at home."

"Does anybody have a daughter like Mary Ellen?" said George Huws with a tear in his honest eye.

Mari Huws would often walk to the door on the morning Mary Ellen's letter was expected, and when it arrived they both feasted on its contents. I have no doubt that God has preserved the joyful tears they both wept in this wonderful girl's favour.

Around this time, Willie Moreton, mentioned previously, was sent to the *Pandy*. The money they received for his upkeep was a substantial help. But above all, having a son after losing one did a lot to fill the emptiness in the heart and mind of George and Mari Huws.

CHAPTER XII

WILLIE MORETON

From the first day Willie Moreton entered the house of George and Mari Huws as their adopted son, they considered him an important responsibility. They strived to fulfil the role of parents as best as they possibly could. As mentioned previously, he received an excellent education, and he strived to use it appropriately. He matured, as we have seen, into an intelligent and affectionate boy, but a consistent and increasing problem to the area. Strangely, the people of Nant y Gro couldn't leave him alone; he was always criticized or idolized by someone or other. Without any effort on his own part, he became the talking point of the area. Some loved him, others loathed him, but nobody forgot him. When there was nothing else to talk about, the weather and Willie Moreton were always at hand. As mentioned already, most of the people of Nant y Gro were related, and they were very suspicious of anyone who dared to come to the area with the intention of staying there. Willie Moreton had no mother or father, brother, sister or cousin in the district; and for all he knew, he hadn't a single relation in the whole world. But one heart in Nant y Gro had been charmed by his personality, and that heart beat for him alone.

"Do these people believe in the transmigration of souls, George Huws?" asked Willie Moreton one day. "I'm sure you know, that some very learned men believed in that type of thing long ago."

"Good gracious, what made you ask such a question, my boy?" replied George Huws.

"Well, I'll tell you. I've just been talking on the bridge to some of the villagers; we weren't all in agreement, and some had nothing better to do than taunt me about my birth, as if I had chosen to be born. From their taunts, I could have thought that I existed before I was born, and that I'm to blame for choosing to come into the world, and especially to this quiet area. I never heard of anyone except Jesus Christ who got to choose his mother and his home. Have you? Do you think it's unreasonable to believe that being born gives someone a right to live?"

"Ignore them, my boy," said George Huws, "when the Apostle Stephen's persecutors failed to reason with him, they could think of nothing better than pick up stones and show their teeth; every age has more brawn than brain."

Willie took his thoughts to the small parlour in the Huws' home, the *Pandy*. This was where their son Robert Arthur used to study, and had been called it the prophet's room in his honour. But Willie couldn't for the life of him concentrate on his book, because on every page he saw the pretty face of the girl he loved. And who happened to pass the window when he was in this condition but Myfanwy, Captain Wiliams' affectionate and elegant grand-daughter.

"*Morannedd*," the old Captain's comfortable home, stood on a hill outside the village. The mountain towered behind it, overshadowing the house, and in front lay the sea. The Captain couldn't be happy without seeing the ocean waves where he had spent so many years.

One had to pass the *Pandy* to travel from *Morannedd* to the village, and seeing Myfanwy, even through the window, was like oil on Willie's wounds.

Myfanwy was a cheerful, pretty girl who never spoke ill of anyone. She had two lively blue-grey eyes, thick blonde hair and an eternal smile.

Everybody liked her. She was the most popular person in the area. She had a good figure, and in addition to this, was exceptionally talented. She was very good at singing and reciting, and no meeting was considered a success unless Myfanwy took some part in it. She was a prominent member of the choir formed by the son of the *Llwydiarth,* and even though Dick Puw, Sam Puw's youngest son wasn't any more of a singer than his father, he insisted on being a member of the choir so he could enjoy Myfanwy's company. Everybody knew that Dick Puw was head over heels in love with Myfanwy - everybody apart from Myfanwy herself, that is. Indeed, many of the chapel people looked forward to the day these two families, who had been on such friendly terms for so many years, would be joined in marriage. But the idea didn't cross Myfanwy's mind. It's true that she allowed Dick Puw to walk her home, but she didn't think any more about it. Catrin Elis, who lived in the chapel house, did her best to further Dick's cause with Myfanwy. Catrin Elis greatly respected Sam Puw and the old Captain, and this was one reason she tried to promote the courtship. Myfanwy used to tell Catrin some of her secrets; she knew she was as safe as the bank.

"I heard that Dick Puw walked you home after choir practice the other night, Myfanwy," said Catrin

Elis, "I hope you're not leading him on; that's never a good thing, you know."

"What can I do, Catrin Elis? I don't want to be rude to him, but he knows full well that I prefer Willie Moreton to him; I can't stop him walking with me; my grandfather and everybody else push him into my company, so what can I do? I want to be honourable."

"It's very important that you try to please your grandfather, Myfi; I heard him say that he'd rather throw his money into the sea, where he earned it, than let Willie Moreton get his hands on it."

"Well, my grandfather can do what he likes with his money, and I'll do what I like with my heart. I know that grandfather can't abide Willie Moreton, and fair play to Willie Moreton, he offered to free me from this torment the other night. He suggested I would be better off financially with Dick Puw than with him. But do you know what, Catrin Elis, I'd rather live on dry bread with Willie Moreton than have all the worldly comforts with Dick Puw – that's the truth, even though I wouldn't tell anybody else but you."

"Well, well, that's always the case with Adam and Eve's family; we want what's forbidden more than what's permitted. If somebody told old Peter Parry that he couldn't come to chapel, or closed the chapel door in his face, he'd come even if he had to climb in through the window; but because he's free to come, he won't. When I told my children not to play with fire when they were young, they were sure to do it. Prohibiting, somehow rouses our opposition, doesn't it, Myfanwy? Do you know, I almost think sometimes that this world would be better without the Ten Commandments."

"I know what you mean Catrin Elis. Maybe I'd get more peace if I was fonder of Dick Puw, but because everyone pushes him onto me, and tries to keep me away from Willie, I hate him and want Willie."

One evening, the Captain and Myfanwy were sitting together in front of a blazing fire. "I don't think I'll go out tonight," said the Captain, "It's a bad sign seeing these seagulls coming inland; there must be a storm brewing."

"Can I take your shoes off, grandfather?" No sooner had she suggested it that Myfanfwy was on her knees, as usual, attending to her grandfather. She reached for his slippers, gave him the matchbox, and the Captain started puffing happily on his 'churchwarden' pipe. Myfanwy saw her chance, and after a careful introduction, she asked: "What do you have against Willie Moreton, grandfather? If you knew him better, you'd think more of him; I feel more virtuous, and far wiser in his company than with anybody else."

The captain drew a puff or two, and got to his feet. "What do I have against him, really – everything! To start with, his parents must have something against him, why would they have disowned him otherwise? Nobody knows who his family are. For all you know they might be the greatest scoundrels imaginable."

"But Willie Moreton can't help that, grandfather; it's not who a man's parents are, but what a man is himself. As Mr. Jenkins said last Sunday morning, Abia came from the house of Jeroboam, and George Whitfield from the Bell Inn."

"God help you, my girl, there's more in blood than you think."

"Well, blood isn't as important as sense! Listening to you, grandfather, you'd think that a man is responsible for his family; but nobody can carry their family on their back. You and I would prefer it if Aunty Catrin's son weren't related to us; but we can't choose our family; even though I wouldn't choose anybody but you as my grandfather."

The reference to her cousin touched the Captain's honour because he held his family in rather high esteem, but the reference to himself softened the blow a great deal.

"You think now, Myfanwy, about Dick Puw. His family are well known in the area. Sam Puw is the chief man in the chapel, and everybody looks up to him. You know, you need common sense when you're courting, as with everything else; you can't live on sentiment when you need to eat and pay the rent. Have you ever seen a nicer lad than Dick Puw? Have you ever seen him absent from the seiat? And a virtuous girl like you should put a price on the fact that he's so useful in chapel. And remember too, that he has a wage. Where will Willie Moreton get money to keep a wife? Sam Puw can provide a comfortable home for his son. Your grandmother and I can give you something, and you can both live trouble free."

"Remember, grandfather, I have nothing against Dick Puw, but you can't direct your love where you want to, like steering a ship. There were plenty of nice girls around when you were young, but I heard you say that you would have been a bachelor forever unless you could have had my grandmother."

"Yes, but remember, Myfanwy," said the Captain

hesitantly, "it's very different for a man, compared to a woman."

"Grandfather, if it's a man's privilege to propose, a lady can refuse; you need two to agree now, as you did back then."

"Yes, but you see, Myfanwy, the idea of marrying an infidel – the thought of bringing a man in to my family who has no respect for religion drives me insane."

"An infidel! Seriously! Willie is a better Christian than half of us. It's a man's life, not his words, that testifies to what he is. Didn't Jesus Christ despise the customs of his days, and wasn't it religious people who crucified him?"

Myfanwy saw that nothing would prevail, and that continuing the discussion was pointless. On a moon-lit night, shortly after this, two people were seen sitting on a stile beneath a grove not far from *Morannedd*. The girl looked bashfully at her shoulder, trying her best not to move, as passionate speech flowed from the young man's lips. "Don't believe them, Myfanwy," said Willie, "I'm not an infidel. No, I can't believe everything that Sam Puw and your grandfather view as important but I can truly say that they are both completely honest, though the prejudice of old age has overtaken them both. Prejudice, backed by a conscience, is the most vicious thing in existence; that's what made Saul of Tarsus so cruel. Honest, prejudiced, religious men are always the cruellest persecutors. Just think how Galileo was persecuted by good men for saying that the earth revolved around the sun; but it's worth having a sun to revolve around, isn't it, Myfanwy, despite the persecution."

"Well," said Myfanwy emotionally, "you're not denying that the Bible is God's word, are you, Willie?"

"Good heavens, Myfanwy," Willie replied heatedly, "no of course not; but these chapel people look at things too mechanically; the Bible, as they view it, has fallen complete from heaven. You'd think that some of them believe that it's been bound there too, but I prefer to believe that it's grown with man. Their belief about the creation of the world is the same; you'd think by listening to some of them that the earth had been put together like a stonemason builds a building, stone by stone, with no living connection between them. Don't you think, Myfanwy, that it's much more natural to believe that creation has grown gradually, and that creative energy is flowing into it today just as it did back then? God didn't put branches on trees, but made them grow; but despite that, the oak tree is just as divine as if it had been created directly. Some people give the impression that God never did anything apart from creating the world and write a book. But God today is as much a fact in the history of worlds and beings as he ever was; everything is constantly evolving. 'Let us make man,' said God, and he's still at it – and man becomes greater each day in the hands of the Creator. God in Himself is infinitely perfect, but he's still growing in mankind and becoming ever mightier. God hasn't finished working, that's the testimony of His incarnate Son; and neither has he abandoned the world. He lights the moon over there, Myfanwy. He paints the flowers, and He inspires prophets in every age. He imprints his plans on souls, yes, on minds; not on parchment and paper; it's men who are inspired, not books."

"But you must admit," said Myfanwy, "that my grandfather and Sam Puw's religion has created excellent characters."

"I'll admit that straight away, Myfanwy. I don't want to belittle the faithful of the chapel in any way, but you must remember that a soul is greater than a creed, and a man is greater than his life. Christianity is also more of a disposition – more of a life than a belief – and a man's experience of the Gospel is often deeper than how he interprets his experience of belief. Man's experience of the salvation of the Gospel is real, nobody can take that away from him, but a man can fail to accurately interpret his feelings and his state of mind. God allows man to experience His Grace, but it is man himself who forms creeds, and unfortunately, men are often more fervent for the man-made creed than the divine nature upon which it is founded. That's the unfortunate thing with the old brothers of the chapel; if I say anything contrary to their way of thinking they call me an infidel. But see now, Myfanwy, God created the sea over there, but man invented sailing. God brought the stars into being, but man created astronomy. Seamanship and astronomy can change, but the stars and sea remain. God created gold, but man coins it and imprints his image onto it. Human institutions can be improved without impairing divine substances in the slightest. It's natural for human institutions to grow and change. Nobody and nothing gets old while they grow, but once anything stops growing, that's when they die."

"But don't you think, Willie, that there's a place for religious customs? I think that we are greatly indebted as a nation to old religious practices and customs."

"Yes, I agree, Myfanwy; I have a deep respect for the old customs, but I don't think any custom or establishment will last forever. Custom has its day; but only truth remains unchangeable, not customs. Water retains its value independent of the channel it flows through. It's not the vessel that quenches man's thirst, but the water. To use the Master's phrase, the vessels can age and become useless, and the wine must be put into new vessels. I can think of a man being zealous for customs. That is, I can think of a man having religious feelings but leading an immoral life. If you think of Peter Parry, he's much more religious when he's drunk than when he's sober. The chapel's everything to him when he's drunk, but you never hear him speak of the chapel when he's sober."

"It's a great shame you don't try to be less offensive to the chapel elders, Willie," said Myfanwy tenderly. "I'm afraid they misunderstand you."

"I assure you, Myfanwy," he said, "that I'm as careful as I can be, without betraying my convictions. Isn't being true to your conscience more important than anything, Myfanwy? I sacrifice my feelings for their sake every day, but sacrifice my principals - never! You have to remember that staying in post for a long time makes men conservative and oppressive despite everything."

The sound of approaching footsteps disturbed their conversation, and they had to part. But periodically they spent hours discussing such topics.

"That's what I like about Willie Moreton," Myfanwy once said to Catrin Elis from the chapel house, "he talks about things worth thinking about. A lot of the chapel people have nothing better to talk about than each other's faults. These people and their faults aren't worth wasting time on in a world so full of the Creator's greatness."

Myfanwy and Willie Moreton's romance became the talking point of the area. I'm afraid that their love, on the whole, got far more attention at Sunday School than God's love towards men. Sara Morus and two other ladies were at the *Fronchwith* one evening entertaining each other, and Myfanwy and Willie's romance was their topic of conversation.

"The old Captain will break his heart if Myfanwy marries Willie Moreton," said Sara Morus. "I don't know what on an earth will become of them, but I know she won't get a penny from her grandfather."

"Isn't it strange," said the second lady, "that she won't take Dick Puw. I heard, and from a very reliable source too, that the Captain had promised her a thousand pounds if she only married Dick Puw. I'd marry my grandfather for less than that."

"That's how it is," said the third. "If I had money everybody would be after me, but everybody knows that my fortune lies in my arms" – even though everybody knew that in her tongue was closer to the truth.

"The three of us have to admit," said Sara Morus, "that there never was a better girl at her work than Myfanwy. You very rarely find so many good things in a girl; she's pretty, intelligent, and good at her work. I'll never forget how kind she was to my mother; she came to visit her every day, and always brought something with her. She's the same with rich and poor alike."

"Yes, to be fair to her, she's a kind enough soul, and come to that, there's nobody kinder to the poor than Willie Moreton, whatever his weaknesses are."

Early in winter a Sunday School meeting was held at Nant y Gro and representatives from the various Sunday Schools in the area attended to question the different classes. When a learned man started questioning the older people about 'the Person of Christ' Willie Moreton couldn't refrain from contributing to the discussion. It wasn't long before he upset the whole class by suggesting that there were limits to Christ's knowledge, and that, being fully human, he grew in knowledge like other men do. He also dared suggest that man's creativity as a free individual has limited the operations of the Infinite one as a Moral Guide, and that God's delay in saving the world was due to man's disobedience, not God's unwillingness. These ideas greatly angered the Sunday School, and poor Willie Moreton was severely criticized, to Myfanwy's great sorrow. Six of the representatives came to *Morannedd* for tea afterwards, and whilst Myfanwy waited on them and poured the tea, her heart bled as she listened to them laying into Willie Moreton.

"You shouldn't put up with him as a chapel member, Captain," said one.

"We've brought the issue to the minister's attention more than once," said the Captain, "but the last time he was here he told us that it's not right to turn someone out of the chapel for having unorthodox views if his spirit is in the right place."

Despite that, the Captain hoped that the event was a stroke of Providence to separate Myfanwy and Willie Moreton, and to improve Dick Puw's prospects.

Almost a year passed; Moreton worked hard with

his books, and Myfanwy remained faithful to him despite all opposition. That year, the National Eisteddfod was held in one of the main towns of North Wales. The residents of Nant y Gro gave very little attention to events that weren't local or to do with religion. There were, however, a few poets and writers in the area who were interested in the Eisteddfod. Even though Willie Moreton was taunted because of his English blood, he was more fervent than anybody in his enthusiasm for the Eisteddfod. The year in question, he was especially interested, as he had competed in the essay competition entitled "The Welsh People's Commitment to Education." Apart from Myfanwy and himself, nobody knew that he had competed. When the Eisteddfod arrived, the author with the pseudonym 'Young Man from the Hills' was deemed the best contestant by far, and the Committee's adjudicators suggested that the essay be published as a book because it was so exceptional. When the winner was called to the stage, a tall, pale young man with a thick crop of black hair stood up and made his way forward with everybody's eyes on him. "What's your actual name," asked the leader. "Willie Moreton from the *Pandy*, Nant y Gro," the young man humbly replied. Most of those assembled had never heard of the young man or his village, but the leader predicted a very bright future for him. In due course, the essay was published as a book, and it was so exceptional that one Member of Parliament suggested it would be wise to have it translated into English. The result was that Willie Moreton from Nant y Gro became a well-known name throughout the country. Myfanwy was overjoyed. She hoped that this stroke of Providence would wean her father off Dick Puw and improve Willie Moreton's prospects.

Willie Moreton's services became greatly called upon. He wrote articles for some of the kingdom's most famous newspapers. He had spent years thinking – gathering honey into the hive; he now had the opportunity to air his thoughts to a wider circle. As he succeeded with his various plans Willie Moreton whispered to himself, "What will Myfanwy think of this?" And on seeing Willie Moreton gaining power and influence, a question pushed itself into Myfanwy's mind, "What does grandfather think of this?"

CHAPTER XIII

SABBATH AT NANT Y GRO

Who of my readers privileged enough to have spent a Sabbath in the countryside can forget the enchanting silence of the old Welsh Sabbaths. It was as if the *Foel*, the mountain that towered majestically over Nant y Gro, had cast a spell of silence over the Lord's day, and the area's conscience permitted no noise at all on that day, apart from ringing the parish bell. Even the dogs of Nant y Gro, either through instinct or strict discipline, seemed to be able to distinguish between a Sunday and the other days of the week; for not even the rowdiest dog would bark, nor the most inconsiderate shepherd whistle on a Sunday. On a weekday, Ezra Griffith was rarely seen coming to the village without 'Gelert', his dog, at his heels. On the Sabbath however, the dog dared not venture further than the farmyard gate. Ezra Griffith was sometimes adamant that Gelert was a devout Christian, and was even of religious stock. His mother – 'Queen' – used to attend chapel twice on Sunday, and behaved as appropriately as one could expect of a dumb animal. Only once in living memory did she overstep the mark, and that was when she tried to join in the singing, and Ezra blamed Mari Jones' screech for that. The simple folk of Nant y Gro made a real effort to keep the Sabbath as a special day.

On a Saturday afternoon it was easy to see that a more important day would follow, because the women would be busy cooking Sunday dinner. Seeing the fresh meat and the pudding bowls in the pantry made us children sigh for Sunday; and what wonder, after living for a week on porridge and flummery, bacon, buttermilk and curds and whey. Remember also that tea and coffee were fairly uncommon luxuries for the small farmers of Nant y Gro back then. It was also interesting to see the women, on a Saturday afternoon, carrying water from the well. They had to make two journeys, at least, to have enough water for Sunday. Even though there was a pump in the centre of the village, it was not very reliable, as it was prone to hysterics, like Anthony Jones' wife, and a hysterical pump is as difficult to handle as hysterical people. Most people therefore went to the well, and many interesting conversations happened travelling back and forth. Some women carried two pitchers, and I remember Maria Owen was a great heroine among the women, as she carried her pitcher on her head, to the great amazement of us children. She had a very unpleasant incident once because, unfortunately, after long service, the bottom of her pitcher gave way, and its entire contents flowed over Maria, leaving both her head and the pitcher in a terrible predicament. It was an unforgivable sin to tease the old lady about her 'second baptism.'

And it wasn't only the women who prepared for Sunday. No, the men could be seen closing the gaps in walls or hedges, and cutting enough hay for the animals until Monday morning. The men cut their beards once a week, and that was a task in itself as their beards were usually more abundant than any acre on their smallholdings. Often there would be very little soap in the shaving box, and no more left in the house, and sometimes the wives had secretly used the razors to remove corns. I saw more than one man in a terrible state about the task, and pulling the most horrific faces. It's very lucky that snapshots were not popular back then, for one glance at them would have scared the crows away. After shaving, many men felt as relieved as if they had returned from the Crimean war unscathed.

The last task of Saturday night was to wind the clock, and great care was taken to wind it forward all the way, as if the owner were in a hurry to see the Lord's day approaching. For many people nowadays, Saturday appears too short, and they are determined to extend it by stealing hours from Sunday. Young people are kept in the shops until midnight to wait for careless religious people to buy their groceries. I'm afraid that a law will be needed to remind the saints of their lack of grace. But the saints of Nant y Gro went to bed early on Saturday night after completing every task punctually, as they believed a tired body would not help them to receive a blessing on God's day.

They awoke early on Sunday to welcome the day, and the children sensed a Sabbatical tone in their father's voice, so they didn't dare speak too loudly. It's true that the old people believed in keeping the home quiet on the Lord's day. They were eager to hear God's voice and God had an excellent opportunity to speak. He scarcely gets that today.

Perhaps some people nowadays think that the old fathers placed too much emphasis on trivial details. For example, one of the old preachers caught his maid peeling potatoes on a Sunday, and scolded her severely. The following Sunday the maid gave him jacket potatoes, and when she saw him peeling them she asked spontaneously, "Is it a smaller sin, master, to peel potatoes after boiling them than before?" The question hasn't been answered satisfactorily to this day. Yes, many prejudices still need to be eliminated, but despite everything, I would say that the Sabbaths of the 'old Wales' had many advantages that the 'future Wales' cannot afford to disregard.

However, if all worldly labour was previously rejected on a Sunday, most people in the district strived to serve the Lord on that day. A good crowd came to the prayer service at seven o'clock, the ten o'clock service, the Sunday school at two o'clock, and also to the evening service.

I was amazed that so many families from a great distance away faithfully attended the morning meeting. Some brought their food with them, and ate at the neighbouring houses. It was amusing to see the hedges on Sunday evening all lit up by the lanterns of the simple old pilgrims of the Nant. On a fairly dark Sunday evening, a few of us had no greater pleasure than climbing a small hill behind the chapel and watching the lanterns coming from many different directions towards the chapel like tiny stars. "Can you tell whose light that is?" one would ask. "I'm sure it's the *Lledrod* family," another would reply. Sometimes the light would disappear behind a hedge, then would appear again, just as a swimmer's head sometimes disappears beneath a wave and later appears on the crest. They would cross streams and stiles. They traversed remote paths: sometimes the fields had been ploughed and their feet sunk in the mud. What wonder they often felt grateful on seeing the chapel's light. By then we would be at the chapel door, second guessing, and welcoming them as a sailor's children welcomes their father's ship back from sea. There would be a lot of bother in the chapel courtyard as people went home. This is what you'd hear by the door: "Light my lamp, my boy, whilst I put my coat on." After preparing for the journey they would climb the hillside like people departing from a great feast, and you could often hear them at the crossroads, before parting, singing the old hymns of the sanctuary together, until the echo of their praise resounded between the hills. Happy days! The memory is sweet as honey.

One of the humblest establishments in Nant y Gro Chapel was the Sunday School. It was even humbler than the Sunday service. At Sunday School people sat together in the pews – servants and masters, rich and poor – whilst at the Sunday service every family sat in their own hired pew. One man was heard at the service, but everybody got to hear their own voice at Sunday School, and enough original sin has remained in us that many of us prefer to hear our own voice than the voices of other people, no matter how respectful we are of the preacher.

The people of Nant y Gro held the Sunday School in very high regard. One of the greatest disadvantages of the old Sunday Schools was a lack of rooms to use. As with all other organisations intent on restoring ordinary people to dignity, the Sunday School establishment suffered from oppression by the landowners. Ordinary people bear many scars from their fight for freedom and equality. Previous generations suffered the disadvantage of having to teach different classes in the same building, but they were unable to secure land on which to build an extra classroom. Because of lack of space, the 'A B C' class was taught in the Great Pew, and was led by Shon Gruffydd and Betsy Puw. It was a wonderful sight seeing the old brother with his bald head and long beard among the little children. He sat them all on his knee in turn to teach them, and Shon Gruffydd's knee was the children's first impression of the throne of grace. To the children of Nant y Gro, Shon Gruffydd's lap was the same as Abraham's bosom for the Jews. Even though he had no children of his own, if you asked most of the village children, "Who's child are you?" the answer as a rule would be "Shon Gruffydd's child."

In addition to Sunday, the children's class also met on Thursday night, so that Shon Gruffydd and the children could have the chapel to themselves. On Thursday night he taught the children to sing the alphabet. It's surprising how well he arranged the alphabet to be sung to the tune of 'Men of Harlech'. In this way he got the older children to teach the younger ones, because they would sing at home what they had learnt, and the younger ones would effortlessly take up and repeat the lesson. Sometimes amusing, even comical things would happen. Once, when the old fellow was questioning the children, one child began questioning him back. The teacher asked: "Who made you, my children?" "God," they replied. And then, one child asked: "Who made Mark Owen, Shon Gruffydd?" "Well, God, of course, my child." "Well," said the little one, "How come he didn't finish him? He has no hair on his head. He's like you with all his hair under his chin." Shon Gruffydd then asked, "How much did Lot's wife lose, my children, for turning back to look at Sodom?"

"She lost a lot," was the suggestive answer. Another time he asked, "Who was the first man?" I don't know whether the child understood the tense of the verb, but he instantly answered. "Huw Morus from *Caehir*. He caught a hare as it was running." Another time, when Shon Gruffydd was questioning the children at the school, he asked: "Who swears, my children?" "Bad people" was the answer he expected, but one little boy replied "Peter Parry." Peter Parry happened to be at Sunday School at the time, and it is said that the little boy's answer had such a profound impact on him that he gave up his wicked habit for the rest of his life.

As you remember, there was a family pew on each side of the Great Pew in Nant y Gro chapel. The mothers' class was held in one of these pews – in the one on the left of the pulpit. I fear the mothers had been placed so close to the children as punishment for being mothers, not unlike the way the Jews used to place the ladies at the front in funerals to remind them that sin had entered the world through them, and through sin – death. However, the fathers' class was at the top end of the chapel, as far away as possible from the noise of the children, as the lords of creation probably had shorter tempers than the ladies.

Yes, the old people flocked to the Sunday School at Nant y Gro. It was wonderful seeing them flooding to the school with their Bibles under their arms. Everybody back then brought their Bibles with them. People take greater care of their own Bibles than borrowed books, and the old people weren't ashamed of their Bibles wherever they took them; they took their Bibles and religion everywhere. The motto nowadays is "leave them in the pew," and many apply the motto to their religion as well as to their books. Sometimes one or two might come without their glasses. When that happened they often asked me: "Will you nip to get my glasses, my boy, they're in the bowl on the dresser." Nobody locked their houses on Sunday. I often undertook that journey, and by the time I returned the school might be in full swing. It was wonderful hearing the sound as I approached the chapel. From one direction I heard a child in class F saying the alphabet, then another child in class A spelling in song. Then a deep sound came from the men's class, like the murmur of the sea, and the sound of the pleasant harmony is in my ears to this day. I have heard a similar medley of voices on threshing day, but not the same harmony. Nant y Gro's Sunday School was like a beehive. If there was noise there was also wonderful honey, and I'm almost led to believe that the noise sweetened the honey. To this day I don't like a quiet Sunday School.

Sam Puw was the teacher in the senior citizens' class, where many intense debates took place. Many a Sabbath was spent trying to correlate God's sovereignty with man's moral freedom; and another time they tried to harmonize the teachings of the Confession of Faith with the Scriptural teaching relating to the universality of the Atonement. There was once a heated debate on: "Should baptism be done by sprinkling or immersion." As it happens, the brother who argued for baptism through immersion had just returned from the asylum, but he was well-versed in the Scriptures. In no time he had gained the upper hand on his opponent, and he, in a week moment, started to taunt his unfortunate neighbour for being insane. The old fellow kept himself composed, however, and answered his opponent calmly: "I have a certificate to prove that I'm sane. I doubt you have one."

Near the fathers' class was the young men's class, under the guidance of Mr. Cunnah. This is where the son of the *Llwydiarth*, Dick Puw, Willie Moreton and the boys from the *Fron* used to meet. Through the diligent efforts of Willie Moreton, Peter Parry, referred to previously, was successfully brought into the school. As well as being a prolific curser, the old brother was also a terrible drunkard. Not a day passed without Peter Parry being drunk. This story will demonstrate how fond he was of drink. A river flowed under the village bridge, and after heavy rain it raged fiercely. As there was a lot of iron in the hills from where the river flowed, the water sometimes looked like beer. Peter Parry was standing on the bridge one day, drunk but not satisfied, leaning on the banister, and he said to the river: "If your taste was as good as your colour, you'd never get to sea. I'd drink you dry." But through Willie Moreton's tireless persistence, Peter Parry came to Sunday School, on the condition that he could sit next to Willie Moreton.

The drunkards of Nant y Gro fled from Sam Puw. They hid in the hedgerows or cowered in a corner when they saw him approaching; but the most terrible characters gathered around Willie Moreton. Whilst many of the chapel's best people avoided him because of his views, his gentle spirit attracted many of the area's shadiest characters. More than one of the area's worst characters attributed their return to religion to Willie Moreton's quiet influence. Peter Parry, in his old age, became a young man, and he insisted on being in the young men's class, 'with the lads' as he said. He experienced a complete conversion. When the minister asked him: "Are you the man who used to be completely drunk in town every Saturday night?" his answer was "I *was* that man, but not any more, thanks to God and Willie Moreton." But even though Peter Parry was completely restored through grace from his corrupt habits, the old prejudices and superstitions of the area remained in him.

Indeed, many of the good people of the area were superstitious. Mari Huws and Beti Wiliam, two godly old sisters, believed in ghosts, and they admittedly preferred seeing *two* black crows than one; even Sam Puw and the Captain connected some sad event with a dog's howling in the dead of night. Sara Morus was adamant that she heard a cockerel crow at an unusual time before the lady of the *Fronchwith* died, and the old shepherd's wife insisted that she had heard a 'corpse bird' knocking on the window the evening her husband died in the snow. Cawrdaf's[11] description of Welsh superstitions is a fairly accurate one of Nant y Gro:

"A howling dog prophesies
that a shroud will soon be needed.
A healthy cockerel crowing
calls a dying man home."

****

"Corpse candles light the paths
leading to the church,
Fate and her hard hand show
that a man will soon be taken."

11   *The bardic name of the poet and printer Wiliam Cawrdaf Jones 1795 – 1848*

When I was a child, I heard a lot about the ghosts of *Coed y Wern*. This is how as children we were unwisely discouraged from being out too late at night. But Peter Parry was a great authority on ghosts and superstition, even though he himself admitted that he saw far fewer ghosts when sober than when drunk. The Sunday School, however, beat many superstitions out of him! Even though the class teacher Mr. Cunnah and Willie Moreton, as a rule, disagreed with one another on various topics, they were both uncompromising enemies of the area's superstitions. For example, whereas Moreton rejected the idea that the *words* of the Bible were inspired, and also believed that not every part of the Bible was equally inspired, both the pupil and the teacher believed that the area's superstitions, and the belief in ghosts, had no Scriptural basis. They both believed that ignorance was the mother of superstition. But Peter Parry was a great believer in ghosts. The issue came up in the class one Sunday, and the old fellow discussed the topic very skilfully. He referred to the fact that ghosts had appeared to Abraham and Lot, and Manoah and Joshua. "But," said Mr. Cunnah, "I'm not saying that ghosts can't appear. I'm saying they can't appear without breaking the laws known to us. If they do appear, it's got to be for some specific reason, and the reason must be one that could not be reached by ordinary means, because whenever God does something, he always uses means appropriate to the aim he has in mind."

"Well," said Dick Puw, "the Devil appeared to Jesus Christ in the wilderness."

"Quite so," said Mr Cunnah, "but there was an important aim, a moral aim, in the instances cited by Peter Parry and yourself, and the aims justify the means in these circumstances."

"I believe," said Willie Moreton, "that we do a disservice to the Bible if we give historical value to things like this. Remember that imagination has its place in the development of the world's thinking. Also, people in ancient times, especially in the heat of emotion, could barely distinguish between the impression made on their mind and external circumstances that would have caused it."

"I don't think you'd believe in ghosts even if you saw one," said Dick Puw.

"I've never seen one," said Willie Moreton, "and if I saw one anywhere I should see one in Nant y Gro. There are plenty of them here, judging by what I've heard from people."

"I've never heard anyone," said the son of the *Llwydiarth*, "whose opinion I value, and whose liver and nerves I believe to be in order, saying that they've seen a ghost. I've walked these paths at every hour of night, and I've never seen anything worse than a bird, or an animal, or a human."

"Well, it's the Gospel truth," said Peter Parry, "I'm sure I saw the Baron's ghost when I was coming home one night from Caerefron. As you know, lads, the Baron's Mansion has been empty for a long time, for thirty years at least, and many people have tried living there, but nobody gets any peace because of the Baron's ghost. There's a terrible racket there at times, and there's a light in the windows some nights, even though nobody lives there."

"Well, yes, but what did you see, Peter Parry?" said Dick Puw. "You're very slow getting to the point."

"You would be as well, my boy, if you saw what I did."

"Tell us what you saw," said two or three in the class.

"Well, I saw the old Baron himself standing in the middle of the road. It was so dark I couldn't see my own hand, and even though he didn't have a candle or a lantern, bright light flashed from his eyes and the night was like daylight – you could have gathered pins off the road."

"Well, you'd probably had a drop too much," said Willie Moreton.

"But despite that," said the old brother, "I left sober as a saint."

And at that moment the president's official knock terminated every class and debate for that Sunday. However, to prove that he was right and that ghosts didn't exist as the area's superstitions led people to believe, Willie Moreton slept for three nights at the Baron's Mansion. Through words and deeds, he spread light that banished 'corpse birds' and 'corpse candles' slowly but surely from the area.

CHAPTER XIV

THE OLD PHILOSOPHER'S SPEECH

It was customary every quarter to address the young people at three o'clock on a Sunday afternoon. Sometimes the minister would do this, but the main hero on these occasions was one of the faithful men of the cause and a teacher at the Sunday School – a man known as 'The Old Philosopher'. This title was given to him by his acquaintances as he was a great thinker. The old brother was a widower and lived on a smallholding by himself. Many of the most intelligent boys of the Nant liked to attend his 'College' as they called it. Even though he was not a gifted orator, everybody listed attentively to what he had to say because he was such an original speaker.

Here is a summary of one of his speeches as written down by Willie Moreton:

"My dear young friends – I want to say a few words this afternoon that will help you to think. The mind is God's greatest creation, and the most similar thing to God Himself. Man was sent into this world to think. The mind is never healthy unless it is working. One of the old writers wrote as follows: 'Try and learn something about everything, and everything about something.' It's very sensible advice, but with all due respect to the writer, you can't know everything about anything. You see, the secret of creation is in everything, meaning you can't know everything about anything –

even about a daisy – because it's the work of a Creator. Everything that grows is divine, and everything in existence is alive. The root of existence is in everything, and everything's roots are in God. Things, you see, are only visible forms of invisible Energy. Life is one, even though it has unending variations. God the Creator unifies everything; that's the reason creation doesn't disintegrate. Have you ever thanked God, not for your senses, but that you live in a created order that makes sense? If a man did not see his image in creation, as he sees his reflection in a mirror, he would go insane."

"Believe you me, my young friends, there is more to know than you can discern, and more to accomplish than you ever can achieve."

"A statement like this shouldn't make you despair, but spur you to begin thinking and working without delay. Remember that one today is better than two tomorrows. I'm afraid that some people spend more time thinking about how to avoid work than it would take to complete it. "

"You will see that there is no time to hang around the village pump whilst there are so many things to think about, and so much work waiting to be done. Wasted time can never be redeemed, and you can only live once."

"And what's more, time will never be more precious than it is for you now. You can live more when you're young than when you're old. The clock over there measures sixty minutes to the hour for everyone alike. But remember, God's time is measured by something more accurate than a clock. The length of every hour depends, not on a dead machine like a clock, but on a living soul. You can squeeze more into the hours when you're young than when you're old."

"Make sure you not only begin your life's work immediately, but that you know how best to complete it. Work is easy and pleasant when you know how to do it. No work will kill you, if you do it in the right way. You may have heard some people say when they're cutting hay, that they cut far less hay than the energy they burn. But they haven't mastered the art."

"I'm sure you've heard the verse: 'He who doesn't work, shouldn't eat.' Here's another verse for you from the book of Experience – the first chapter and the first verse. 'He who doesn't think, shouldn't work either.' The thoughtless worker damages not only himself, but his work too, and it would be cheaper to keep a man like that in the workhouse."

"Do your best in everything; yes, stamp your work with the image of your soul. A small ring can be as round as a big ring. A creator, according to the nature of things, must create everything in his own image. Don't do shoddy work. Strive to do good work instead. Be enthusiastic in your work: enthusiasm awakens imagination, and the imagination is a creator. Some people are like an oven, warm enough to burn things but not hot enough to bake anything. You know of men like that. Oh! I would like to see you, my boys, enthusiastic enough to imagine things that will benefit society. Watt saw more through a kettle's spout than many of us have seen through a large chimneystack! Who of us have never seen an apple fall from a tree, but Newton discovered a law when he saw an apple falling. How foolish, indeed, it is to waste your time on futile things.

I heard a young boy the other day boasting that he had won first prize – for writing a verse of poetry to a flea! He would be much more of a man had he invented a trap to catch it. Invent something that will benefit mankind; don't be satisfied living in other people's light."

"Don't complain about your lot – overcome it. Life, remember, becomes empowering when you overcome difficulties. Money can't buy muscles, and neither can pedigree form character – they are both fruits of labour. A dead fish goes downstream with the current, but it takes a live fish to swim against it. Show that you're alive, my boys. It's folly to expect success without work and troubles; don't trust in this thing called luck. The law of cause and effect ensures that effort brings success in all fields. If you have any faith in God, believe in work. Often, the greatest disadvantages will be your best friends; nobody reaches the heights without climbing."

Remember to associate with intelligent young men. Believe the old saying 'arguing with a stupid man is as foolish as suing a poor man.' You can't afford to spend your time, any more than your money, on anything or anybody that doesn't bear fruit."

"Know, my young friends, where you are heading, and make sure you know how to get there. Strive to return to God greater than you left Him. Don't grow up into men too soon, but take care that you don't remain children for too long either. Every one of us came into the world as a little baby, and I'm afraid that some people leave this world as big babies."

CHAPTER XV

THORNS AND FLOWERS

W hat on an earth kept you so long in that chapel tonight?" Beti Wiliam asked her husband, Owain Wiliam, when he returned home from an elders' meeting at Nant y Gro Chapel one dark and stormy night. Beti Wiliam couldn't refrain from asking, even though she knew that questioning someone like they did in Sunday School was not a very effective way of getting anything out of her husband. On more than one occasion she was heard saying, "You'll get nothing out of Owain through questioning him, and it's very foolish to question a man with an empty stomach. If you need to find out something from a man, look after his belly." That was Beti Wiliam's philosophy, and she understood her Bible and human nature pretty well. On the evening in question, she saw on her husband's face that something significant had happened. Even though he tried to appear indifferent, his face was too faithful a barometer to hide the signs of a storm, and Beti's instincts were too accurate to fail, as women's instincts generally are.

"What's wrong tonight, Now?" asked Beti directly, addressing her husband by his pet name.

"I'm sure there's more thorns than flowers in this world," said Owain Wiliam sadly. "I find it hard to believe sometimes that the same God created things so different as thorns and flowers."

At that moment Beti Wiliam brought a bowl of porridge and warm bread out of the oven. "Eat this, Now, and you'll sleep like a top after it, despite them." The old fellow turned to the bowl, but he had very little appetite. Beti noticed that he was playing with the spoon, furrowing his brows like somebody deep in thought. The old lady knew that it was futile to question him under such circumstances, so she picked up her knitting needles again and started to sing gently, -

"The Cross is not forever carried
O deliverance."

As the old man ponders over his simple supper, allow me to paint a picture of the old sister. Beti Wiliam was a jolly old lady, with a round, moonlike face. She was the same height and width; she was too round to be measured with a two-foot ruler and you would need a piece of string to measure her accurately. But if her body was round, so too was her character, without any corners in it.

She had been blessed with the ability to see, on the whole, the bright side of every cloud. She saw a star in every night, and that was often an advantage for her melancholy husband.

"It's a shame you've lost your teeth, grandma, isn't it," said her little grand-daughter once when she saw her having great difficulty trying to chew a pickled onion. "You've only got two teeth left, haven't you, grandma," she said with heartfelt emotion.

"Well, don't you worry, Olwen," said the old lady. "The two I have are opposite each other. It could be worse."

Another time the old lady had put her best shawl

out to dry on a thorn bush near the house. Unfortunately, the cow wandered past and ate parts of the shawl. Her little grand-daughter ran into the house shouting excitedly, "Grandma, grandma, come out quickly. 'Blackan' is eating your shawl." But instead of complaining about the damage done to her shawl, she said "Thank goodness that the cow didn't choke." As you can see, she was gifted with the ability to look at the bright side of everything; and it was very fortunate for Owain Wiliam that his wife was so different to him. The old fellow often came home from a rather contentious elders' meeting threatening never to go again, but his wife's optimism and joyful spirit would soothe his turbulent feelings before he went to sleep.

"Well, Now, are there more thorns than flowers in that porridge? It's going down very slowly," said Beti Wiliam. "Don't you think, seriously now, that you should allow us women to be elders? I think there'd be less arguing and much more work."

"Ha! I'd like to see you women trying to handle Anthony; you'd be lucky to come home alive," said Owain Wiliam.

"Oh! So Anthony was at it again tonight, was he?"

"Yes, of course he was, in his worst mood; he starts every argument. I've never seen a thorn like him."

"Was everybody else all right?" asked Beti.

"Yes I suppose so."

"Well, remember then, Now, that there are more flowers than thorns even in an elders' meeting. But that's how we are, focusing more on one thorn than on many flowers. People remember one rainy day better than ten sunny ones."

"It's easy for you to talk like that," said Owain Wiliam. "Good sense tells you that there should be no
thorns at all in God's church."

"You're spot on, Now," said Beti, "but it should be
some comfort for us to remember that there are more
flowers than thorns in the church. The Great Master
suffered one Judas because he had eleven decent men."

"Do you know what, Beti, I find it harder to understand how Judas was able to stand Jesus Christ, than
how Jesus Christ was able to stand Judas. I don't know
how such a bad man was able to live for three years with
someone so good without burning. The light hurts week
eyes, and the good should trouble the bad. Think how
painful it would be for a fish to be on dry land. If Anthony doesn't like his position in the chapel, why doesn't
he resign and join people of his own kind?"

"God help you, Now," said Beti, "the world
wouldn't put up with half of the trouble he causes you.
What was his problem tonight?"

"Well, you know how Amos, Anthony's lad, is
behaving."

"Yes, I know," said the old lady. "I told them many
times when they were choosing a name for him that no
luck would come from the name of one of the minor
prophets."

"Tut, tut, Beti, that's got nothing to do with it, but
this is what I wanted to tell you: just think of Anthony
daring to accuse two old Christians as good as Sam
Puw and Shon Gruffydd that they were to blame that
his son doesn't attend chapel any more. The Captain

spoke rather plainly with Anthony, but he said it exactly as it was. 'What surprises me, Anthony Jones,' the Captain told him, 'is that your son stayed so long in chapel when you and your wife do nothing but criticize it. No preacher or elder satisfies you and no service is to your liking, but remember, you damage your son far more than you damage the cause.' 'Me criticizing the chapel?' said Anthony excitably. 'Who told you that?' 'Well, since you're asking, your own son told me that he hates the chapel when he hears his parents arguing about it at home.' At this point Anthony lost all control of himself and flew into a rage, and nearly everybody walked out. I don't remember anything else, only Shon Gruffydd's tears and Sam Puw's serious, pale face.

When he knelt down before going to sleep that night, Owain Wiliam offered up a heartfelt prayer for Anthony and his family, and Beti's 'amens' flew like sparks from the intensity of her feelings.

Anthony Jones left the same meeting, but there was no Beti Wiliam to calm his raging temper. Before his wife had any opportunity to question him – and she never lost the opportunity to do that – Anthony Jones poured out his hard thoughts in the presence of his wife and son, and received all encouragement from his wife.

"You did the right thing," said his wife. "You don't have to take anything from those scoundrels; I'll go to see the old Captain tomorrow, and tell him how many days there are till Sunday, you just watch me. Our Amos can do without advice from him and his sort. I'll make sure Amos never goes near their chapel again; we won't give a shilling towards the chapel, and that will settle them, you'll see. We don't look as stupid as we are."

"Not as stupid as we look, you mean," said Anthony.

She was true to her word, despite the loss to herself and her family. Amos matured, and went from bad to worse, and Anthony and his wife hardened under the circumstances. It was one thing for Anthony Jones to sow seeds of hatred in his son's mind, but reaping the fruit was more bitter than he expected.

Before Amos was twenty-seven years old, he fell out of a carriage when he was drunk. He injured his head when he fell, was paralysed, and his senses were affected. For years he was too alive to be buried, and to dead to live. Willie Moreton visited him regularly; nobody else could understand anything he said as his speech was incoherent. He could say "Sam Puw" relatively clearly, but he couldn't say 'mam' – Sam Puw was everything.

About two years later, adversity visited Owain Wiliam's house. Beti Wiliam was taken ill and she languished in tremendous pain for months. However, the deadly pain in her breast did very little to darken her serenity. Despite this, she was sometimes plagued by the fear of death.

"I don't know what on an earth to think of myself," said Beti Wiliam to Sam Puw and Shon Gruffydd when they visited her. "The fear of death has overwhelmed me. I'm ashamed of myself, you see. I've professed religion for over fifty years and here I am afraid of one of my Lord's servants. Will both of you please pray for me to be released from my fear. I don't fear damnation, but I'm scared of dying. Pray that I may be released from the fear of death."

This is what she told everybody.

Many prayers were said for her in the chapel and in the homes, and sure enough, the prayers were heard. This is how she related the story to Sam Puw. "The other night I was praying and meditating alternately. Suddenly I saw Jesus Christ, and even though I've caught glimpses of him many times before, I've never seen him as he was that night. There was some kind of divine smile on his lips, and a mesmerising charm in his face. He was compelling me to come to him, and I was eager to go. But I remember that there was an old river between me and him, and I thought I heard the sound of its cold waves. I stepped back in fear, and he continued to beckon me to approach him. At last I dared take a little step, and I noticed that he too took a step forward at the same time; I took another step, and yes, he took one too. On seeing him approaching me, his steps matching mine, I became more confident and brave, and I took bigger and quicker steps, and yes, he did exactly the same. I forgot everything about the river of death and rushed into his arms, and Oh! I felt the most wonderful feeling in my whole life. It's worth suffering this illness to enjoy that feeling, and it will be worth dying to realise it. When I found myself safely in his arms, I asked, 'Lord Jesus, where did the river go?' He smiled sweetly at me and said 'There's no river where there's faith; doubt creates a river, faith dries it up.' Owain Wiliam insists that I was dreaming, but I'm telling you, Sam Puw, that I was as awake as I am now; but dreaming or not, the fear has gone, and I can now say 'Even so, come, Lord Jesus.' Will you tell them at the seiat, Sam Puw, that there's no river of death?"

The old lady had a wonderful respite from then until the end. The people of the chapel flocked to see her, and everybody felt better after being in her company. She died victorious.

The following Sunday, the old brother Huw Elis, the announcer, rose and said. "There will be a vigil tomorrow night at Owain Wiliam's house, and the funeral procession will leave the house at two o'clock on Tuesday." The vigil was a very popular custom in the area. When two o'clock arrived, people crammed into the kitchen and the pantry, and some people sat on the stairs leading up to the loft. Owain Wiliam sat in his oak chair beneath the chimney, surrounded by his closest relatives. Everybody was crushed with grief that night. A round table covered with a white cloth stood in the centre of the room, and on it were two brass candlesticks and the Bible. Sam Puw started the vigil very effectively. Even though he was a sensitive man, he kept himself strictly composed, but Shon Gruffydd broke down completely. Many friends from the area came to offer Owain Wiliam their condolences, and everybody brought a gift, as was customary in the area.

At funerals, food was provided for those present. It was sometimes said that some people went to funerals more for their bellies than to sympathise with the bereaved. I know that one old brother earned himself the name of being one of the disciples of the loaves.

"What kind of funeral did the lady of the *Gelli* have?" one old brother asked him once.

"Huh! I'll never go to bury *her* again; I didn't get half enough to eat," said the old brother innocently.

I remember my mother saying that funerals had improved greatly within her lifetime in this respect.

"In the old days," my mother said, "there was plenty of beer at every funeral. Lots of tobacco and pipes were put on the table, and those who smoked would help themselves. Before leaving the house, lots of glasses were placed on the table, and two ladies went around, one with glasses in her hand and the other with a jug, and everybody would get a glass of beer before starting. When the service had finished, the parson and the mourners would all go to the Crown, without exception."

The vigil survived in the area until very recently, but it pleases me to think that the drinking stopped at respectable funerals many years ago.

Beti Wiliam was given a very worthy funeral, and many people beside Owain Wiliam felt that there was one less flower in the area. However, her departure caused a beautiful flower to blossom.

On the way back from Beti Wiliam's funeral, Willie Moreton had an opportunity to speak to Sam Puw, Shon Gruffydd and Mr Cunnah. After discussing the old sister's virtues, and the loss to the church following her departure, the conversation turned to Anthony Jones' family.

"Will you forgive me for asking you one favour, Sam Puw," asked Willie Moreton.

"What's that, my boy?"

"Would it be too much for me to ask you to visit Anthony Jones' troubled family. They are worried sick about Amos, as you know, and nobody from the chapel has been there for months."

"But remember, Willie Moreton," said Mr Cunnah, "they left the chapel of their own accord."

"Quite so," said Moreton, "it's a painful thing to see a family turning their back on the chapel, but it's a tragedy to see a church – the church of the Saviour – turning its back on a family."

"Well, to be honest with you, Willie Moreton," said Sam Puw, "I'm afraid that I wouldn't be given much of a welcome if I called."

"Perhaps, if you'll permit me to say this, Sam Puw, that's more of a reason for you to visit. Often, where we're most unwelcome is where we're most needed, and it's need, not welcome, that should appeal to us most."

"But remember," said Mr Cunnah, "there's another side to the question. People must think something of you before you can be of much benefit to them; you can't do people any good if they simply don't want that."

"Forgive me, Mr Cunnah, but does not the Holy Spirit convince us despite all else?" said Moreton.

"But if you think," said Mr Cunnah, "of how faithful Sam Puw and Shon Gruffydd, and everybody else from the chapel come to that, have been towards Beti Wiliam."

"Well, yes," said Moreton "I've heard a lot of good things about both of them, and about you as well, Mr Cunnah, but permit me to say, without being too forward, that it was easier for Beti Wiliam to die without your help than it is for Anthony Jones to live without it;

but I'll admit, that everybody prefers handling flowers than thorns."

"But you must remember that Anthony Jones and his family have been nothing but trouble for the church for years, that you can't expect us to go much out of our way." said Mr Cunnah.

"Well," said Moreton, "If one family can do more damage to a church than a church can do good to a family then it's scarcely worthy of its Divine Founder. It's one thing to make the good better, but it's another thing, equally important in my opinion, to turn the bad into good. A church should make it difficult for thorns to grow, and easier for flowers to spread; and if the world will not come to the church, then the church must go to the world, and disturb it. The return of one sinner, says the Great Teacher, causes more joy than ninety-nine just ones."

"Do you have any basis to believe, my boy," asked Sam Puw gently, "that my visit would be of any benefit? I've suffered a lot from Anthony and his family, but when I think of how much Jesus suffered for us, there's nothing too much for me to do on His account."

"Well, Sam Puw," said Moreton, "I'm unwilling for anyone to go to perdition without doing everything I can to prevent it. And another thing, you can do no harm to anyone by showing that you're eager to help him. And apart from that, I wouldn't like to think that the church has turned its back on anyone whilst the Master's gaze is still on him. 'For to him that is joined to all the living there is hope.'"

On this, Willie Moreton departed, and the three elders went to Sam Puw's house for a cup of tea. However, Willie Moreton's request had disturbed Sam Puw, and he asked, "Shon Gruffydd, will you come with me to Anthony's house?"

"Well, yes, of course, I'm afraid that Anthony's had a terrible few months in his cave; there was a lot of good beneath his fiery temper."

Both agreed to go there before the seiat the following week, and so it was.

They received a very cold welcome. Anthony's wife was extremely distant, but Sam Puw realised that they had both aged considerably during the past months. But if Anthony and his wife tried to appear cold, the moment Amos saw Sam Puw he threw his arms around his neck, and as he couldn't speak, he made up for it with kisses. This event had a profound impact on the family. They saw that the man they had slandered so ruthlessly was their unfortunate son's idol. After a long chat and much quoting of Bible verses by everybody, the two elders got on their knees, and Anthony Jones and his wife followed suit. It was easy to see that the chapel had a hold on them, but that they were too obstinate to submit. However, Sam Puw and Shon Gruffydd left with much more peace of mind, and believed that the visit had answered its purpose.

As the two elders were heading from Anthony's house towards the seiat, they heard great shouting and the sound of people running, and they discovered that the dear old chapel was on fire. Even though they were both greatly advanced in years, they ran as fast as they could. The whole village rushed to help. The fire was coming from the direction of the chapel house. Some people ran towards the village pump, others towards the well, and others to the river, and a great effort was made to extinguish the fire. Anthony Jones worked harder than anyone, as if there were enough tears of repentance in his heart to extinguish the flames if they could all be amassed together. He rushed to meet the flames with more daring than anyone. The flames seemed to be receding, and the water doing its work. There was room to believe that one part of the chapel could be spared. When Anthony Jones saw that the flames were receding, he rushed into the chapel to try and rescue his mother's great old Bible that he had long neglected. He reached the old pew, took the Bible, but at that moment one of the beams fell on him and he was severely injured. He was unconscious for many hours. When he came around, he asked for Sam Puw and Shon Gruffydd to come one each side of his bed. In their presence he vowed to be a better man from then on, and he insisted for the vow to be written on his mother's Bible that was saved from the flames.

"Well, my little brother," said Shon Gruffydd, "the gain is more than the loss; it was worth losing the chapel to save a soul."

Everybody noticed that Anthony had changed completely. Previously, he found fault with everybody; but now, after removing the beam from his own eye, he looked at everybody much more benevolently. What wonder the Old Philosopher made the following comment: "The King of Heaven is a clever one, isn't He. He took a beam from the chapel's roof to knock a beam out of Anthony's eye." Naturalists say that birds who stay at home and suffer the coldness of winter sing the sweetest when spring comes, and that this is why the thrush's song is more melodious than the cuckoo's. Similarly, Anthony began to sing a new and sweeter song after this misfortune.

The damage to the chapel was less than initially thought, but for many months the congregation had to worship in the *Tyddyn's* barn. A great deal of time was spent discussing the question: Would it be better to repair the old chapel or to build a new one? Most of the old people felt it would be wiser to repair the old chapel; whilst the young people felt very eager to have a new chapel. But the difficulty was getting enough land, especially from the Baron's reluctant agent. However, help came from an unexpected source, as we shall see in the next chapter.

CHAPTER XVI

SHADOWS AND SUNSHINE

Crying is a valuable asset to a child. Otherwise, he would be deprived of many of life's legitimate pleasures. A child must make himself a nuisance before he gets his rights. It's not children that impersonate men when they strike, but men that impersonate children. But this method suits a child more than it does a man, because the former only has his lungs as a weapon, whilst the latter can rely on his brain. The instinct behind a child's crying, however, is infallible. I'm not suggesting that I was wiser than my peers when I was a child, but I discovered very early in life that I got many things by crying and shouting that I would never have otherwise. My mother sometimes went out and left me at home in bed or under a neighbour's supervision. I discovered that the only way to avoid such an injustice was to cry with all my energy, and my mother quickly realised that she had no chance of going anywhere without taking me with her. I'm indebted to this gift for being able to attend Aunty Margiad's wedding. Even though I was only very young, the event left a profound impression on me.

We set off early in the morning by carriage to Caerefron; in the front with Robin the driver sat Joe Huws the musician. He played the crwth[12] as we passed each house, probably to publicise the marriage. And you

---

12 The crwth is an old Welsh folk instrument similar to a violin.

should have seen my aunty that day. I had seen her
feeding the pigs and doing various other similar tasks
wearing clogs and a sack apron, but she was exceptionally smart on her wedding day.

She was dressed in a grand blue gown, flounced
from top to toe, with a wide crinoline train like a peacock
spreading its feathers. A silk paisley shawl was draped
over her shoulders and on her head was a finely quilted
cane bonnet, as was fashionable back then. There was
a pretty box on the front of the bonnet, and in it was a
bouquet of the prettiest red flowers my eyes have ever
seen. She was extremely pretty. I thought that my aunty's
boyfriend, Uncle Wiliam as I came to know him later,
had been very fortunate in his choice of a wife.

My father also looked very swell indeed in his
velvet waistcoat, breeches, tweed leggings and ivory
buttons. My mother had terrible trouble with his high
white collar and bow tie, and had great difficulty persuading him to wear them. Whilst the white collar was
not very comfortable, everybody was looking at him,
and I was proud of him.

As Nonconformist chapels were not licensed
back then, Nonconformists were forced to attend the
church for their weddings and funerals. That's where
my aunty got married. After the service, we went to my
grandmother's house. I noticed that Robin, the driver, was not half as steady on the way back. Thankful-
ly, however, the old mare was wiser than Robin, and
fortunately for us knew the way home. A huge feast
had been prepared at my grandmother's house, and after eating, everybody danced the 'cushion dance.' Joe
Huws played the crwth passionately, and the young

couple knelt on a cushion in the centre of the room, and the guests danced in a circle around them. That was the last time I saw 'the cushion dance' because the religious revival took hold soon after that, and these customs were banished from the neighbourhood.

I was led to tell this story because word spread in Nant y Gro that one of the area's young men was about to get married. This revived the memory of my aunty's wedding. Yes, that was the story in the area: "Have you heard that he's going to get married." They never said "she". Of course, it takes two to get married, but that's what everybody said. "*He*'s going to get married." "I wonder how he'll provide for her." Nobody was allowed to name him, but everybody knew who he was. It's very unfortunate in a wedding if 'she' in emphasised more than 'he'. If 'he' isn't somebody before getting married then, well, poor fellow.

"I'm sure more men are getting married this year than women," said one of the area's well-known bachelors. It's probably the emphasis on the man in the prospective marriage that brought this idea to his mind.

It's strange how interested old people are in the relationships of young people, and especially in their marriages. I've heard that Sara Morus would have married the man of the *Fronchwith* years ago if some busybodies hadn't interfered. "People are so nosy," said Sara Morus to the lady of the chapel house. "Some people would cause a dog to argue with its tail if they could."

But whilst rumours of Willie Moreton's marriage filled the air, something else happened that occupied the residents of Nant y Gro for a few months. On a dark, stormy night a large iron ship was washed ashore.

She was blown so high up the beach that she was left on dry land when the sea receded. It's true that the sea surrounded her sometimes, but not enough for her to float. Many treacle barrels were part of the cargo, and to make the ship lighter they were thrown on the beach. The children from the Nant and the surrounding area had a lifetimes supply of treacle. It was on their faces every day, treacle is a great betrayer.

After the large ship had been on the beach for many weeks, word spread that Captain Wiliams had bought it for a few hundred pounds. If he succeeded in getting it out to sea when the high tides came in, rumour had it that it would be worth thousands. Many experienced sailors believed he would succeed; and everybody rejoiced thinking that the captain would see to rebuilding the old chapel of Nant y Gro when he came into his fortune. That was the area's opinion of the Captain's generous nature. But, whilst everybody was rejoicing thinking of the fortune that awaited Captain Wiliams, one heart in the area was worried that the prospected thousands would make it more difficult for him to take Myfanwy as his wife. "If the thousands go to Myfanwy," he whispered to himself, "will she take a poor lad as a husband?"

The Captain spent a few hundred pounds preparing to get the boat out to sea when the high tide came. A huge trench was dug in the sand, appropriate tugboats were hired, and every possible effort was made. At long last the day dawned! Here comes the long awaited high tide, rushing in with great force and raising everybody's hopes with it. The sea has surrounded the large ship. The strong tugboats begin to pull. Hopeful prayers rise from many a breast. Hundreds have gathered on the beach. The crowd thought at one point that the ship was actually moving, and let out a fanfare of applause. The Captain's fate is at stake: if the ship sails – thousands; if not – poverty. He was unsuccessful this time, but some believe that if the wind continues to blow the tide will rise higher still, that tomorrow will be more hopeful. The following day arrived, but brought disappointment with it. Instead of gaining thousands the Captain lost everything! The whole area was distressed, and sadness spread through the district. However, one heart saw the failure as almost a success. Willie Moreton was glad thinking that he could now take a poor girl to be his wife, and he took comfort in the hope of being able to welcome the disappointed old Captain to live with him and Myfanwy. He promised himself that the old Captain would never be in need as long as he lived.

Willie Moreton didn't have to doubt Myfanwy. No, her heart beat faithfully for her true love. What was wealth for her next to her lover's affection! Her love was constantly directed, like a sailor's compass, towards the same point. There was unquestionable evidence for that. Had not the son of one of the wealthy owners of the ship been staying at *Morannedd* for weeks. He was charmed by Myfanwy's beauty, and offered her his hand; but her heart answered to nobody's advances, only to the charm of the alluring young man who had already won her affection. However much Willie Moreton loved Myfanwy, she loved him with equal passion.

The old Captain had to sell *Morannedd* and everything else he had in order to meet the costs of his unfortunate venture. They were forced to leave the old comfortable house and move to a modest smallholding. The Captain threatened to go to sea again, but the work and worries of past months had affected his health. Help came to him in the generosity of his old friend Sam Puw; he proved to be a brother in a time of adversity, and the flame of friendship continued to burn brighter than ever. Sam Puw was not a man to abandon a friend in the heat of the battle. No, he stood by his friend like a rock. The months rolled slowly by, and Myfanwy cared unceasingly for her grandfather, despite him being a shadow of his former self.

On October the 21st, 18—, the notice below appeared in the Times:

"We deeply deplore the death of the Hon. John Moreton of Bedford Hall, Norfolk, after a severe and protracted illness. Burial will take place at the family vault on Wednesday," &tc.

What has this got to do with the quiet, tranquil area of Nant y Gro? Wait one minute.

Thirty years prior to this an affable and beautiful young girl from Nant y Gro went to England. She was her parents' only daughter. Even though she had received very little education, something in her speech and demeanour made her nobler than most. The neighbourhood gradually forgot about her because she never visited her place of birth after burying her mother and father. She went to work as a domestic servant for a noble English family, and eventually worked as a housekeeper for the John Moreton mentioned above. He was a widower with one son named Edmund.

After she had been there a few months Edmund fell in love with her, but because of the difference in their social status, and as they knew how zealous his father was to preserve their family traditions, their love was kept secret.

However, when the respectable old man was visiting the continent, they married on the understanding that the marriage was to be kept secret, at all costs, whilst the father was alive. They both succeeded in this respect. The birth of their only child posed a problem, but that was taken care of. The child was given a comfortable home with George Huws in the *Pandy*. Not even George and Mari Huws knew who his parents were, as the boy was taken there by a friend of the parents who had been rearing him until then.

But, when the old gentleman passed away, the barriers were removed, and Edmund Moreton used all means possible to unveil the situation. Willie Moreton was declared the legitimate son of Edmund Moreton, Bedford Hall, Norfolk. This of course meant that he was the heir to a vast inheritance in England on his father's death. Willie Moreton was shocked when the secret was revealed to him, but more than anything else he was relieved that he was his mother and father's legitimate son. After the taunts he had endured all his life, after the suggestions thrown at him, he was far more satisfied with this fact than with all the wealth he was to inherit. Of course, this was now the talking point of the small area of Nant y Gro. A few months ago the question on the village's lips was – "I wonder if Myfanwy will take Willie when her grandfather makes his fortune?" Now, the question was; "Poor Myfanwy, there's no chance Willie will take her as a wife when he's from such a noble family and an heir to so much wealth."

When Myfanwy heard that the young man who

had been disregarded by the area for so many years was from such a prestigious family on his father's side, and was by now a man of wealth and status whilst she was a poor girl in the shadows, she decided to write to him to release him from all promises made.

"The poor boy, who was persecuted so terribly, and who I fell in love with, does not exist any more," she wrote. "He has been exalted and I have been humbled. I can live now with the sweet memory that I once won your love, and that I was true to the covenant made between us under the grey light of the moon on that unforgettable night. My love has not died; in fact, I want to release you because I love you. I know that you will now be obliged to move among the most prestigious people in the country. You can choose a wife from whichever circle you wish. I can only wish you all the best," &tc.

Myfanwy's simple letter pierced Willie to the depth of his soul. He still loved Myfanwy, and he rushed to the modest smallholding to assure her that his heart belonged to her completely.

"Myfanwy my love," he said, with the flame of true love shining in his eyes. "I would rather have your heart than all the world's treasures. I didn't desire wealth, it came to me, as you know, unexpected, but I chose you, and you've inspired me in everything that's good since I first knew you. Far from dampening my love towards you, Myfanwy, the worldly privilege that's become mine has intensified it. To me, there's no meaning or value in them without you."

Willie Moreton's parents unsuccessfully tried to persuade him to forget about the quiet area of Nant y Gro, but he insisted on being near Myfanwy, no matter what.

When his parents saw that their efforts were futile, his father agreed, on Willie Moreton's request, to buy him Baron Owain's estate. Willie had become enchanted by the Baron's Mansion, with its glorious park and fertile gardens, since those three nights he slept there to drive away the ghouls. The mansion was splendidly renovated. In due course, Willie Moreton and Myfanwy were joined in holy wedlock, in a simple and unpretentious ceremony, as they both wished.

Willie Moreton managed to persuade the old Captain to come and live with them in the Mansion. He agreed, on the condition that he was taken regularly to Nant y Gro chapel. One of the first things Willie Moreton did after acquiring the Baron's estate was to re-build the worthy old chapel. He also built a convenient and healthy schoolroom to teach the children, and a cosy chapel house for Wiliam and Catrin Elis.

Willie Moreton didn't forget the poor he had fought so hard for. He tried to teach them to foster an independent mind, and not to live on charity. He strived to improve and develop them in all aspects, and helped them to the best of his ability. He even veered slightly from his usual belief and built a row of excellent almshouses for the elderly people who lived in unsuitable houses, and endowed them in perpetuity.

Even though his circumstances had changed, he remained the same. He spent his time and money to lessen the burdens of poor workers, and to ensure better educational advantages for their children. Myfanwy accepted the promotion without losing her head. She turned the old mansion, which was once the home of oppression and a lair of ghosts into a refuge of mercy and house of generosity. Willie Moreton visited the *Pandy* every day, and cherished "the prophet's room", as it was called, as God's Sanctuary.

Now, his status helped him to transform the area with his ideas. He awoke ideals in the children of Nant y Gro, and the tranquil area became famous for the children's talents and the innovations of the residents.

As time passed, Willie Moreton was encouraged to stand as a member of parliament, and was successful in that endeavour. Few people today realise how indebted we are to Wiliam Moreton M.P for the improvements we enjoy. He joined forces with a few others to champion the rights of Nonconformity, and he brought the legitimate complaints of the working class before the parliament and general public many times. The improvements enjoyed today are the result of the self-denial of brave men like Willie Moreton, who fought for our cause when blind prejudice, the oppressions of the landlords, and the greed of the wealthy was rife in the country.

Willie Moreton would easily admit that he was indebted to Nant y Gro chapel for everything worth taking pride in, even though he often held very different views to the leaders of the cause. For years he was plagued by doubts, but he confessed that Mari Huws' experiences in the storms of life were too divine to explain without Jesus Christ. When he doubted Christ's influence on men like Peter and Paul two thousand years ago, he was forced to explain a problem much closer to home: how could he explain Sam Puw and Shon Gruffydd without Jesus Christ? He saw that they had been saved by a Divine Personality, not by their ideas. He said many times "I can't help but think highly of Nant y Gro, because that's where Myfanwy was brought up, and while the Nonconformist churches of Wales continue to produce such pure characters, nobody can doubt their authenticity or their divine right to exist."

Do you see that white-haired old man, sitting on the sun-kissed lawn in front of the Mansion, with a baby on his knee? That's the amiable old Captain. The greatest joy of his old age is gazing at Myfanwy in her baby's eyes.

THE END.

alanroberts 1941
@ gmail . com

72893115R00104

Made in the USA
Columbia, SC
02 July 2017